Dearest Dacha

Norman Maclean

D0494030

BIRLINN

First published as *Dacha Mo Ghaoil* in 2005 by Clàr
This edition published in 2011 by
Birlinn Limited
West Newington House
10 Newington Road
Edinburgh
EH9 1QS

www.birlinn.co.uk

ISBN 978 1 78027 006 7
eBook ISBN 978 0 85790 059 3

British Library Cataloguing-in-Publication Data
A catalogue record for this book is available from the British Library.

Designed and typeset by Iolaire Typesetting, Newtonmore
Printed and bound by Bell & Bain Ltd, Glasgow

To
Calum MacKinnon
and
Davie Walker
and
Duncan MacNeil
for whom I first wrote this story as a radio script

Contents

1

The Godfather and the two fools

At the Askernish turn-off in South Uist, Calum Mac-donald violently wrenched the steering wheel of his little van to the left and took the turn at thirty miles an hour. Six and a half feet tall, twenty-five years of age, he was dressed from boots to cap in camouflage gear. His teeth were bared and his shoulders hunched over the wheel. He stamped on the brake pedal and halted about ten feet from the front door of a house that had no roof.

'God be round about us,' said Davy MacIsaac. Twenty, thin, untidily dressed, he slouched in the passenger seat. He stretched out his hand and killed the engine. He threw the keys into his companion's lap. 'Come on,' he said, 'Duncan's expecting us.'

Davy knocked on the door. He stood perfectly erect, listening to the noise of a hammer on metal and a woman's voice speaking in a foreign language with a man's voice responding to her. About a yard behind him Calum sat astride a child's bicycle. 'Davy,' he said, 'what the fuck's going on?'

Davy turned and smirked. 'He's got a woman with him.'

Calum roared, 'Open the door, you dirty little man.'

'Maybe this is a bad time for Duncan,' Davy said.

The door opened, revealing Duncan carrying a hammer. A heavy-set little man, approaching fifty, he wore a white shirt with the sleeves rolled up above his elbows and a pair of jeans that were too tight. Sawdust speckled the crotch. Little remained of his black, thinning hair. A smile came to his face when he saw Davy. 'My very good friend,' he said, 'good to see you.' He frowned when he noticed Calum. 'And . . . you've brought this guy along? You'd better come in.'

From the discarded rubbish lying throughout the room – lengths of copper piping, electrical cables, planks of wood – it was clear that Duncan was in the process of refurbishing the place. The three of them stood awkwardly staring at one another.

'Calum's the name,' Calum declared, stepping in front of his companion. 'Where's the bird?'

'Bird?' Duncan said. 'Oh, right. That's a tape. Trying to learn a little bit of Russian.'

'That'll be handy, Tiny,' Calum said, 'when you're trying to buy a carry-out in Creagorry at closing time Saturday night.'

' "Duncan" around here,' Duncan said. 'You can call me "Duncan" in here. Lads who work for me call me "Mister MacCormack", but you can call me "Duncan". That'll be all right.'

'I'll try to do that, Tiny,' Calum said. 'I'll do my very best.'

'You could've got someone else, Davy,' Duncan said.

'This guy's getting up my nose. I've got to put up with shit like this?'

'I could've got someone else,' Davy said, 'but you asked me, you know, get somebody absolutely fearless. Calum here, he's pretty cocky, but, really, he'll go through a house on fire if it comes to a fight.'

'Personally,' Duncan said, 'I'd like someone who'd see that the house was on fire and walk round it.'

'I've got excellent eyesight, Tiny,' Calum said. 'All I can see in front of me just now, Tiny, is a little squirt, and I'd think nothing of giving him a good clap on the ear.'

'I really don't like this prick,' Duncan said. 'How about going over to Eriskay, Davy, see if you can get me a good-looking kid with dark hair? This halfwit's so offensive I don't want to tell him what I want.'

'For God's sake, Calum,' Davy said, 'won't you shut your gob till we hear what work he's offering us?'

'What I fancy doing,' Duncan said, 'the two guys I pick to do it, they'll get two thousand pounds each. But this one, I don't want.'

'Remember MacLean?' Davy said.

'MacLean? Which one?' Duncan said. 'Sorley, the poet? That clown, Norman Maclean? There are hundreds of them about. Which MacLean?'

'Killer MacLean, Eochar School,' Davy said.

'That bastard, yeah,' Duncan said, 'the guy who nearly killed me the time he caught us smoking.'

'He's not working there now,' Davy said.

'Glad to hear it,' Duncan said. 'I hope he died.'

'He very nearly did,' Davy said. 'Saw him on the pier at Lochboisdale the night he escaped from Uist. He was missing an ear and both his arms were in plaster.'

'Wow!' Duncan said.

'Him,' Davy said.

'You don't say,' Duncan said.

'Kicked him, jumped on him and leathered him.'

'Took a chunk of his ear off with my teeth too,' Calum said.

'He gave you the belt too?' Duncan said.

'He tried,' Calum said. 'I was in Second Year at the time. One day, me and Patrick Michael's son were up the back of the class nipping at a bottle of rum we got in our lunch hour from the Co-operative. Heard the roar: "MacKinnon and Macdonald, out to the floor". Asked me to put my hand out, palm upwards, brought the belt down and I grabbed hold of it and dragged the bugger out into the playground. Never went back to the big classroom, though.'

'He's my man,' Davy said. 'He's hard to get on with, but nobody between Carinish and Ludag can fight like him.'

'Old MacLean was never the same after our little fight,' Calum said. 'He's in a nursing home in Glasgow now, I heard. May not remember his own name these days or even where he put his glasses, but every time he has to turn up the sound on the television because he's so deaf he remembers Calum Macdonald.'

'Is this guy still drinking?' Duncan said. 'Both you guys getting ripped?'

'Oh, dry my perspiration!' Calum said. 'Davy, you been at the shandies?'

'Holy Mother,' Davy said, 'will you shut the fuck up, Calum? No, can't even buy a pint with the money I've got.'

'No drinking,' Duncan said. 'Davy, I asked you to find somebody for me and I've got this job takes two guys, and all they've got to do is do it and we get a nice chunk of money. We're not playing at this thing, you know. I want the money. That's what I need.'

'Tiny,' Calum said, 'I've been drinking since I was in the cradle. When I was cutting teeth the old lady used to give me the dummy-teat dipped in whisky. I'd be lying in the pram, not a tooth in my head, but I was happy.'

'Oh, sure,' Duncan said, 'but I don't want you to be happy on this mission. I want you to be sober.'

'He'll be all right, Duncan,' Davy said.

'Maybe,' Duncan said. 'Want to be sure. I don't want to rush into this.'

'Tiny, you're doing this for the money, right?' Calum said.

'Too right,' Duncan said. 'Love I can get at home. Well . . . occasionally.'

'Duncan,' Davy said, 'I need money. It's a year since I left the uni. I haven't earned a penny since. Delay a thing too long and it's forgotten.'

'My friend,' Duncan said, 'my wife, Isa? She was at the uni. Department of Folklore, you know? She worked there for eight years. She'd been down there in Edinburgh five years before we got married. One time I asked

5

her why she'd never published a collection of Angus Macdonald's poetry – she'd been collecting stuff since she was at school. She told me, she said, "Duncan, do you know how long Alex Archie, the department head, and Margaret, that Harris dame who never ever delivered more than a dozen lectures to the students each year, took before they finally published a tape of the songs of Mary MacPhee? Twenty-four fuckin' years!"

'So, I'm goin' to be just like the academics this time. I'm goin' to bide my time. Phone me Wednesday. Wednesday, I'll know. I'll let you know then.'

Duncan turned his back on them and switched on the electric drill.

2

Go for the rifle

In the front seat of the van Calum and Davy sat motionless without talking, as far from each other as possible, staring at the ruined house.

Finally Calum spoke. 'Right, what you goin' to do?'

'Suppose,' Davy said, 'I'll just head for home . . . well, my sister's home.'

'Please yourself,' Calum said. 'I'm goin' up to Polochar. I've got a meeting there at four o'clock. After that, I'm calling on a French bit of stuff I met last night at Liniclate School.'

'I've got a meeting at four o'clock too,' Davy said. 'With *Postman Pat*. No wonder the folk at home think I've turned queer.'

'Why don't you go down to Benbecula to the school there?' Calum said. 'The place is jam-packed with young things from all over Europe. All you have to say is you know where the corncrake's nesting and they're round you like flies.'

'That's easy for you to say,' Davy said. 'I'm a bit shy around women these days.'

'Och,' Calum said, 'I've been chasing women ever

since Lazarus finished his nap. Lack of practice, that's your problem.'

'How do I get down there without wheels?' Davy said. 'Well, the brother-in-law has an old wreck of a bicycle right enough, but even though I got a loan of it, and I doubt I would – he's a real tight bastard – by the time I got to Benbecula from Boisdale the corncrake would be off on holiday to Tenerife. And I'd be so knackered I'd need a holiday in Tenerife myself.'

'Well,' Calum said, 'I think I'll be taking off shortly myself. Give it a month or two, something like that, if me and Tommy keep at this thing we've got going for us just now, I'll have a new van – refrigerated, boy – and I'll be selling venison to the Germans.'

'Wish I had some of that energy myself,' Davy said. 'Seems to me I spend most of my time arguing with Alina and her man. When I was at the uni down in Glasgow, I used to think, boy, if I ever get out of this fuckin' place, the girls back home better watch themselves, you know? Know what? The only thing that's hot in my life just now is my hairdryer. And that fucker's broke.'

'Go for the rifle,' Calum said. 'We'll get into these stags on Eabhal. I'll get rid of Tommy. He's only a dirty Proddy from North Uist, anyway. We'll sell venison in Germany. They can't get enough of it.'

'Aw, thanks, Calum,' Davy said, 'but I was never in the army like you . . . though I have travelled on Cal-Mac ferries a lot. And I'm a really poor shot. That's why, this job Duncan's got, I don't know what he's got in mind, but it's the only thing I've got in front

8

of me right now. I've got to listen to him.'

'I was willing to listen to him,' Calum said. 'He just didn't want to talk in front of me. He kept looking at me the way Samson must've looked at Delilah when she told him she was thinking of giving him a little trim. Fuck him, he doesn't like me. Okay. But I'm not goin' to be licking his arse just so's I get a big pay-packet from him.'

'Aren't you the lucky guy!' Davy said. 'You don't want the two thousand. Well, I do. And I don't know anywhere else to get it. You do, though.'

'Yeah,' said Calum, 'but he didn't say, he didn't tell us how we were goin' to get the two thousand pounds.'

'Duncan's straight enough . . . in his own way,' Davy said.

'Straight my arse,' Calum said. 'Tiny MacCormack's so twisted he can't lie straight in his bed.'

'Does that mean,' Davy said, 'you're not coming in with us, then?'

'Look,' Calum said, 'go and meet the guy. See if you can find out what he's got in mind. I'll be around. You find out, and you think it's worthwhile, makes no difference to me. You decide you want to do it, that's all right with me, I'm with you. He doesn't want me, I'm out. Doesn't matter to me.'

'I'll go to his house on Wednesday,' Davy said.

'You do that,' Calum said. 'Now will you get the fuck out of the van, or are you goin' to sit there and have your period again?'

Davy got out of the van. He walked down the track. The van overtook him, engine screaming.

9

3

Duncan's plan

Davy stood in Duncan's home in Garynamonie. The man of the house was poking a screwdriver at some piece of electrical equipment in the corner. The Russian tape was playing quietly in the background.

'Duncan,' Davy said, 'why don't you turn that bitch off?'

'You'd better get used to that kind of chat,' Duncan said as he switched off the tape recorder. 'You're goin' to hear a lot of it very soon.'

'What'd you say?' Davy said.

'Never mind that,' Duncan said. 'You're up for this thing, who else are we goin' to get?'

'Your man's up for it too,' Davy said. 'He said if you wanted him, he'll do what you want. If you didn't want him, it wouldn't bother him, he's doing all right as it is.'

'I don't know,' Duncan said. 'The kind of guy I'm looking for, he's got to be more of a ladies' man. Anyway, I don't know if he's single.'

'Single?' Davy said.

'That's it, unmarried,' Duncan said. 'Somebody like yourself who doesn't have a woman giving him grief

10

every single day of his life, talking through her nose because her mouth's all worn out.'

'Neither of us is married,' Davy said.

'How do you know,' Duncan said, 'he didn't get married to some mouth-breather one time when he was drunk? Didn't he try something like that when we were over in Tralee selling T-shirts at the Festival?'

'"Death Before The Free Church",' Davy said. 'That's what was written on them. Didn't sell one. I didn't have anybody to help me. My mate's locked up in the bedroom with that tinker dame – what was her name again? – Mirren, that's it, for a whole week. He had sex with her, I'm sure, but he didn't marry her. He'd a lot of things on his mind that week, that's all.'

'He needs more,' Duncan said. 'A fine claw hammer alongside his head, for example.'

'This isn't goin' to be . . . umh, violent, is it?' Davy said.

'No, no, kid,' Duncan said. 'You're goin' to have a nice time – "honeyed kisses" and all that . . . Listen, have you been with a woman since you came home?'

'Since I came home?' Davy said. 'The most excitement I've had has been getting a haircut from the barber.'

'The two I pick have got to be single,' Duncan said.

'Duncan,' Davy said, 'Calum's single. I'm single . . . and I'm goin' to be, I keep on like this, till I have a beard down to my knees.'

'Still not got any work?' Duncan said.

'You know what I did?' Davy said. 'I went down to the

11

DWP. Skinny prick from Inverness writes down everything I say, what'd I do at school, at university, my entire life story. I happened to mention VSO – Voluntary Service Overseas, you know? "Here's something you could try," he says. "Teaching agriculture in East Timor. Ten grand a year. That's if you last a year. A lot of dengue fever and malaria about." That's enough of that. Then I meet Calum. He's doin' all right, though. Wouldn't be surprised if he buys Uist Builders or something in a couple of weeks or so.'

'Uh uh,' Duncan said, 'it'll take him to next New Year to get two thousand pounds for venison. Oh, right enough, he's got a promising career ahead of him – as a homicidal maniac.'

'Maybe,' Davy said, 'but he'll make it sometime. Me, I'll be sprawled in a chair looking at dots through clouded eyes. For the love of God, why don't you tell me what it is you've got in mind?'

'Ostriches,' Duncan said.

'Ostriches?' Davy said.

'This is the new thing that's arrived in the islands,' Duncan said. 'Ostrich rearing. Huge demand for ostrich steaks in all the restaurants down in London.'

'Really?' Davy said.

'Yeah,' Duncan said, 'they take about twenty years before they're ready for slaughtering but they're worth real money then.'

'For some reason,' Davy said, 'that information doesn't make me feel ecstatic, you know, Duncan?'

'Come here, till you see the plans I've made for the

croft in North Uist,' Duncan said. He reached for a roll of paper on a shelf and smoothed it out on the table.

'I don't know if I'd fancy ostrich steak, Duncan,' Davy said. 'On top of that, I don't know how to go about feeding these beasts. What do they eat? Nails?'

'Forget the fuckin' ostriches for the minute,' Duncan said. 'Look at this. This is where the jacuzzi will be, in the original house as it were, you know? These are the benches all around the walls where the folk can relax. Upstairs, you have the gallery that runs right round the entire room where the spectators'll be . . .'

'Hold it,' Davy said. 'What do you mean? What spectators?'

'. . . and in the extension over here,' Duncan continued, 'that's where the bedrooms will be . . . video, PCs with DVD and MP3 files, en suite toilet . . . Oh, they'll never want to leave once they see where they're goin' to be working.'

'Who?' Davy said.

'The girls,' Duncan said.

'What girls?' Davy said.

'The Russian girls from Novosibirsk,' Duncan said.

'I know I'm goin' to regret this, but what have I got to do with the Russian girls?'

'You're goin' to get married to one of them,' Duncan said.

'I am?' Davy said.

'And that wild man, if he's the one you want, is goin' to marry the other one,' Duncan said.

'You're not goin' to come in?' Davy said.

13

'How the fuck,' Duncan said, 'am I goin' to marry a Russian chick when I'm married to Isa already? I don't want to get married again. I got married once. Once's enough for any guy who hasn't lost his marbles. Quentin and Soraya, they'd get confused with another mother too. Well, more confused than they are. They'd have to go for counselling. Fuck that.'

'What do we get?' Davy said.

'I told you already,' Duncan said. 'There's four thousand in it, if Tanya and Tamara arrive in Uist with papers that prove they're married to UK passport holders.'

'Right,' Davy said. 'I'll do it. With Calum. How much time do we have?'

'The girls are already in Glasgow,' Duncan said. 'They're doing lap-dancing in a pub down there. You guys'll have to go down there a week today. I'll give you the name and address of the man who's looking after them until they get all their papers. I'll start on the crofthouse on Monday, permits'll be through sometime next week. You'll stay in Glasgow for, say, a month . . . in the bosom of Mother Russia.'

Davy spoke in a slow drawl, 'Talking about Russian bosoms . . . you think a guy could . . . you know?'

'You could, kid,' Duncan said, 'if they let you. But don't think you're goin' to get near them when they come to Uist. They'll be far too busy in Strumore . . . looking after ostriches . . . and stuff like that, know what I mean?'

14

4

On the ferry

Davy and Calum walked into the bar of the *Lord of the Isles* ferry. They sat at a corner bench fronted by a little round table a good distance from the three or four other passengers in the place.

'She looked gorgeous,' Calum said, 'absolutely gorgeous. Long blonde hair . . . and you should've seen the size of her tits . . . Fancy a dram? Good job I asked that tight bastard for expenses, eh?'

'A hundred pounds each,' Davy said. 'Not bad.'

Calum looked up as a waiter delivered a plate of eggs, black pudding and ham to the table. 'Good on you, lad,' he said, and immediately began to eat greedily.

'Think I'll have a glass of brandy,' Davy said, getting to his feet.

'Vodka for you, boy, from now on,' Calum said, speaking with his mouth full. He cleared his plate and lit a cigarette and slowly inhaled the smoke. He started to sing softly. He had placed his feet on a stool beside the table when Davy returned carrying two bottles of beer and two glasses of vodka.

'There you go,' Davy said, placing the drinks on the table. He raised his glass. 'Cheers.'

'Cheers,' Calum said.

Davy inclined his head. 'Right, man,' he whispered, 'tell me about the French chick.'

'You still haven't pulled, have you?' Calum said.

'No,' Davy said, 'but I'll have . . .' He took a piece of paper out of his wallet and glanced quickly at it. 'I'll get . . . Tamara tomorrow night.'

Calum sighed. 'What a dumb shit you are! I'll have to ask your mother some questions. She let you fall out of the pram when you were a baby. Maybe she threw you out of the pram. You're so simple you embarrass me, you know?'

'How?' Davy said.

Calum grasped Davy's hand and squeezed it tightly. 'Listen. When you had the motorbike, did you have the helmet to go with it?'

'Yes,' Davy said.

Calum released his friend's hand and raised his index finger as though about to deliver a sermon. He spoke in a deep voice. 'You should have kept the helmet, and worn it . . . every time you went out the door. You've scrambled your brains with all the blows to the head you took. Do you really think you're going to spend the night with one of these Russian girls?'

'Sure,' Davy replied innocently. 'Why not?'

Calum shook his head. 'This business isn't about sex,' he said with a snort of derision. 'We marry them, they get the papers they need and they'll go off to stay . . .

they'll live with folk they know for a week or two. Then, the Godfather'll get word to us and the four of us'll go home to Uist and we get two thousand pounds each.'

'Oh, right,' Davy said. 'Right.' His expression changed; he smiled. 'Well, I know what I'm goin' to do with the money.'

'Tell me,' Calum said.

Davy became excited and began to speak rapidly, spluttering slightly. 'First thing I'm goin' to get, a caravan – my own place, know what I mean? The odd time I've got lucky and nipped some slack-jawed bird at the disco. But, God, it's hard to be romantic when you take a bird home to a house with a mob of kids. The last one, she looked at me like I was a retard when she saw the Lego pieces scattered about the floor. Had to pretend it was my hobby.'

'Well,' Calum said, 'one month from now I'll have a refrigerated van and that's me off to Germany. I pick up the big money there, maybe I'll visit Amsterdam on the way back . . . and buy something there.'

'I haven't finished yet,' Davy said. 'I'll get a motorbike too, an old wreck that I'll do up myself, some new clothes, and then I'm goin' to get myself a girlfriend.'

Calum drank from the bottle and wiped his lips with the back of his hand. 'That French chick I was with?' he said with a wry grin. 'I've never seen anything like her in bed. But she's dangerous.'

'Tell me where she lives,' Davy said quickly. 'Don't go back to her. Don't want you getting involved with a

17

dangerous woman. I'll visit her and I'll read the New Testament to her or something.'

'I didn't say I wasn't goin' to go back,' Calum said, trying not to reveal his impatience. 'I said she was dangerous.'

Davy pretended not to hear. 'I don't think you should go back,' he said. 'Why bring trouble on yourself? Business-type like yourself? Turn her over. I'll look after her.'

'Davy,' Calum said, 'the French bird, she's only fifteen.'

Davy's eyes widened and he waited a couple of seconds before opening his mouth. 'Uh-uh, that puts another complexion on it, then . . .' he stuttered. 'I can see the peasants from my village coming after me, everyone armed with a pitchfork like in those old films about Dracula.'

'Cheer up, kid,' Calum said as he got up to get another drink, 'let's see what happens at the wedding a fortnight tomorrow, first. Lights! Camera! Action!' He began to sing: ' "You're surely getting married to her, she loves you . . ." '

5

Accident at a wedding

At two o'clock in the afternoon in an elegant room in a building in Park Circus, Glasgow, a group of people, male and female, were seated comfortably in leather chairs. They talked quietly, some in Russian, and from time to time would cast nervous glances at the odd couple who stood with their backs to the congregation.

Standing beside Tamara, a big, blonde Russian girl wearing black trousers and a white singlet, which displayed broad shoulders and sinewy arms, Davy MacIsaac, who was at least half a foot shorter than his bride-to-be, looked like an adolescent schoolboy.

All conversation stopped when an old man, completely bald, got up and teetered towards a kind of lectern and faced everybody. He wore a cheap suit that was far too tight on him and carried a bible. He started to recite the marriage vows. Finally, he said, 'And by the powers invested in me . . . I pronounce you, David, and you, Tamara . . . husband and wife.'

The boy's eyes bulged. He seemed to faint. Tamara put an arm round his waist and Davy raised a hand feebly to keep her back. He emitted a series of squeaks and hit the floor with a loud thump. A woman screamed.

The fat little registrar spoke. 'You may now . . . well, pick your husband up off the floor.'

'Give him air,' Calum kept screaming. 'Give him air.' He held the hand of Tanya, his new wife in a grip of iron. They had undergone the marriage ceremony some time before.

'*Nyet*,' Tamara said as she knelt and tried to loosen the collar of his shirt. 'Wodka, Wodka.'

'Good thinking, Tamara,' Calum said. 'I'll have a large one.' He looked around him. 'Somebody give me a hand here? Any able-bodied volunteers to carry my friend over to the dressing room?'

'No need,' Tamara said in a deep, husky voice. 'I carry my husband.' She thrust her arms under her husband's armpits and, grunting and snorting, dragged him across the wooden floor, the heels of his shoes bouncing.

'Holy Mother,' Calum said as he followed them with his mouth wide open, 'what a peat-cutting crew this dame would make!'

A lock clicked as the dressing-room door was closed. Outside in the main wedding chamber muffled shouts and people moving around could be heard.

'Davy,' Calum whispered, 'Davy, wake up, man.'

Tamara bent and proceeded to administer a series of slaps to Davy's cheeks.

Davy started to moan as he slowly regained consciousness. 'Mmmmmm. What happened? Where am I?' Two seconds went by. 'Aaaaaargh! Aaaaaargh!'

'What the fuck's wrong with you?' Calum said.

'That's her, that's her! Fuckin' whore!' he screamed at Tamara. 'Get her out of here! Out! I'll suffer the dengue before I look at her ugly face. Get rid of her, Calum. I'm begging you.'

'Take it easy, kid,' Calum said. 'There, there. You'll be fine, Davy.'

'I go now,' Tamara said. 'Sign documents.'

The sound of high-heeled shoes moving away was heard.

'Last time I saw an arse like that,' Calum said, looking at her, 'was from the back of Jimmy MacKinnon's cart with Rosie the Clydesdale pulling it.'

'Haven't you seen her face?' Davy said. 'Jesus, that's Don't Watch Alone stuff!'

'What'd scare me is how strong she is,' Calum said. 'Wouldn't she be a good hand at putting the shot at the South Uist games in Askernish?'

'God save me,' Davy said, 'she's got hair on the back of her hands.'

'Never mind just now how hellish she looks,' Calum said. 'She's your wife and we've got to get her . . . we've got to get them both home to Uist.'

'The sooner the better,' Davy said.

'Now, my man,' Calum said, 'you've got to go into the Registrar next door and sign the papers he has for you.'

'No fuckin' way,' Davy said, 'I don't ever want to see that . . . ugly big hulk of a woman again.'

'Two thousand pounds, Davy,' Calum said.

The connecting door was opened, and then closed. High heels approached then came to an abrupt halt.

21

'Dah-vee?' Tamara said.

'Mmm, mmm, mmm,' Davy said, a hint of tears in the whimper.

'Come,' said the Russian hulk. 'Come with Tamara.'

Davy sighed and said, 'Okay.' He rose unsteadily to his feet and followed Tamara, Calum trailing behind them.

6

Dalliance or business?

On Friday night, 29 October 2010, at half past eleven, Margaret MacCorquodale, leaning against the gate that led to her father's house in Grenitote in North Uist, watched the approaching lights of a Land-Rover. She was thirty years old and of medium height. She weighed eight and a half stones. She had red hair, cut short. Over tight, just-right trousers and black boots with stacked heels she wore a thick white sweater.

The Land-Rover halted.

'About time too, Harris boy,' Margaret said.

A window was wound down.

'Margaret?' the driver said. 'Margaret MacCorquo-dale?'

This was MacAskill. He was short, forty years of age, around five feet six, thin – he weighed about nine stone. Not much was left of his brown hair, and what there was was grey.

'Who else would it be at this time of night?' Margaret said. 'Shania Twain? I'm the Factor's daughter.'

The passenger door was opened. 'Jump in.'

'You're late,' Margaret said. 'It's almost midnight.'

'Sorry, Ms MacCorquodale,' MacAskill said. 'Phone rang just as I was leaving home.'

'That's okay,' Margaret said. 'I won't charge you for my time . . . on this occasion.'

'And what do you charge as a rule?' MacAskill said.

'Twenty-five pounds an hour,' Margaret said.

'Is that right?' MacAskill said. 'Twenty-five pounds?'

'That's the rate,' Margaret said. 'Fellows uglier than you, they had to pay sixty.' She paused for a second and looked him straight in the face. 'Just kidding.'

'Oh, you're just . . . right,' MacAskill stuttered. 'Are you engaged? Married?'

'God help me, no,' Margaret said. 'What about you? Married? Kids?'

'No, unfortunately,' MacAskill said. 'I mean . . . I'm married, but Mary was never blessed with kids.'

'How old are you?' Margaret said.

'Forty,' MacAskill said. 'And you?'

'Younger,' Margaret said.

'Well,' MacAskill said, 'I'm Alex MacAskill – personal secretary to Lord Granville.'

'Oh, my!' Margaret said, pretending to be impressed by the information. 'Margaret, daughter of Alasdair son of Donald.'

'There's something funny,' MacAskill said, 'there's a weird carry-on taking place in Strumore.'

'I heard that,' Margaret said. 'Ostriches and Russian women, something of that order, eh?'

'Well,' MacAskill said, 'it's the women . . . their behaviour, know what I mean? They're the ones

24

that're causing the man himself the most worry.'

Margaret said, 'The girls are running a . . . How to put this delicately? These are naughty girls, the ones that are working in this house, right?'

'Right,' MacAskill said. 'And they're up to their . . . they're up to their necks in work. As soon as it gets dark, cars and buses packed with men and boys are constantly shuttling up and down.'

'This is happening every night?' Margaret said.

'Well,' MacAskill said, 'that's what was happening last night when I was there.'

'What were you doing there?' Margaret said.

'Oh,' MacAskill said, 'you know, one thing and another. The man himself had heard rumours that this kind of thing was happening, he told me he was worried, and, yeah, I thought, I'll go there myself.'

'You enjoy it?' Margaret said.

'Ye– well, no,' MacAskill said. 'The place is too cramped. It was full of Lewis and Skye men. And they never left a drop of drink for us. They drank the lot.'

'Of course,' Margaret said, 'strong drink isn't what attracted you to the place.'

'Well,' MacAskill said, 'they played videos and CDs there too.'

'What did you watch?' Margaret said.

'It was kind of funny, actually,' MacAskill said. 'They were supposed to be showing a film with an English actress, Mary Poppins?'

'I doubt very much,' Margaret said, 'it was Mary Poppins you saw.'

'Must have been somebody else, then,' MacAskill said. 'Like I say, I forget the name. *Titanic*? *Launching the Titanic*?'

'*Titanic Toni*?' Margaret said.

'I don't know,' MacAskill said. 'Whoever it was, I didn't see much of her. The Skye fellows were all standing up and shouting and the guys from Lewis were singing along with the singer on the CD.'

'Who was the singer?' Margaret said.

'Murdani Mast,' MacAskill said.

'Aye-aye,' Margaret said. 'What happened next?'

'Tanya and Tamara came out,' MacAskill said, 'and they put on a . . . umh, show.'

'What is a "show", Mr MacAskill?' Margaret said.

'God!' MacAskill said. 'You know, it was a show with two women together.'

'I don't know,' Margaret said. 'Tell me what it was like. Is it something I'm missing?'

'Well,' MacAskill said, 'Murdani was giving the "Anchor Bar" song big licks and they had this big tub on wheels full of mud. And the women jumped in and started to wrestle.'

'They just wrestle?' Margaret said. 'Men pay money to see that?'

'Ms MacCorquodale,' MacAskill said, 'they didn't have a stitch of clothes on.'

'Okay,' Margaret said, 'now I'm hearing you. The women are stark naked.'

'I didn't actually see that much,' MacAskill said. 'I was sitting at the back, near the door, you know?

They were naked. I saw that much.'

'You want to be careful,' Margaret said. 'Some fine night I'll get drunk and I'll give Mary a ring and tell her you're never away from Dearest Dacha in Strumore.'

'It was research I was doing,' MacAskill said. 'Well, what's the next step? What do you think?'

'I don't know enough about this business yet,' Margaret said, 'to do much thinking.'

'There's some kind of tie-up,' MacAskill said, 'between them and guys from Uist.'

'We'll see,' Margaret said. 'First of all, I'm going to speak to the designated tenant of the croft – Kirsty, daughter of Angus, son of Allan. She's in Trianaid just now. I'll take my grand-aunt Jean along with me when I go to visit her tomorrow.'

Margaret opened the passenger door, stepped nimbly out and closed it with a sharp bang.

MacAskill started the engine. He wound down the passenger window. 'Margaret?' he said.

'Yes?'

'Do you mind,' MacAskill said, 'if I say something to you?'

'Go ahead.'

'Not only are you very attractive,' MacAskill said, 'but you've also got a very high opinion of yourself.'

'I know,' Margaret said, 'and I don't mind you saying so at all.'

7

Old age comes not alone

In Carnish, North Uist, there is a residential home for the elderly called 'Trianaid'. On Saturday morning Margaret and Jean, a bent old woman using a walking stick and with too much make-up on her face, spoke with a nurse.

'She's in the lounge, is she?' Margaret said. 'Oh, I see her now. Thank you.'

'You're welcome,' the nurse said. She turned and walked away.

'Come on, Jean,' Margaret said, 'till we say hello to Kirsty.'

'Don't fancy this place much,' Jean said. 'And I don't like Kirsty either.'

'We won't stay long,' Margaret said.

'That's good,' Jean said, and when she arrived at the chair where the old woman was slumped she roared, 'Kirsty! I'm so glad to see you. How are you, darling?'

'I'm at death's door,' Kirsty said. 'Who do I have here anyway?'

'Jean, Wee Lachie's daughter from Kallin,' Margaret said. 'You used to be neighbours at one time.'

'Kallin?' Kirsty said. 'I can spit further than that. And who are you?'

'Alasdair, son of Donald's daughter,' Margaret said.

'The Factor,' Jean said.

'Don't know him,' Kirsty said.

'Sure you do,' Jean said. 'It's to him you pay the annual rental for your croft.'

'I don't pay a penny now,' Kirsty said.

'How? Margaret said.

' "Can't get blood from a lump of peat",' Kirsty said. 'That's what the boy from South Uist told me to say if anybody wanted money from me.'

'The boy from South Uist's a lump of peat?' Jean said. 'Who called him that?'

'Never mind the peat, the pair of you,' Margaret said. 'Who's this fellow from South Uist that's become your adviser, Kirsty?'

'All I ever call him is Tiny,' Kirsty said. 'His surname's MacCormack, I think.'

'MacCormack?' Jean said. 'That's a funny name.'

'Now, Jean,' Margaret said, 'why don't you let me speak to Kirsty?'

'Miss Macdonald and Miss Maclean won't let you speak in school at all,' Kirsty said.

'Huh?' Margaret said.

'I know,' Jean said. 'When I was going to Carnish School I used to be a right chatterbox and Miss Maclean sat me between two brothers from Claddach Baleshare . . . Camerons they were, if I remember right . . . And I used to just gaze at them in horror

29

and wonder why they weren't speaking at all . . .'

'You haven't changed much, Jean,' Margaret said. 'Now, shut up for a minute until I find out about Tiny.'

'Oh, he's very nice,' Kirsty said. 'He came to get my autogram in the spring, and I don't care that he's Catholic . . . The truth is, he showed me more kindness and love than . . .'

'Some of them are fine right enough,' Jean said. 'I remember one boy from Eriskay I used to know before I got married – Iagain was his name. Went to sea. Gosh, he was handsome . . . black hair and brown eyes . . . and when he smiled he was as shy as a young boy . . . red lips framing large white teeth, and you'd see his plump tongue whenever he licked his lips . . .'

'We all know, Jean,' Margaret said, 'that you went through the men like . . . like . . . like a lawnmower. Now, let Kirsty tell us about the South Uist man.'

'If you do get married, girl,' Kirsty said, 'make sure you pick a kind of ugly man. Ones that are half good-looking, they think their piss is wine.'

'Shame on you!' Margaret said. 'Stop talking about men. The right one hasn't been born yet.'

'My Tiny is a proper man, though,' Kirsty said.

'Why was he wanting your autogr– umh, autograph, Kirsty?' Margaret said.

'He wanted proof,' Jean said, 'that she went to school, I suppose – that Miss Maclean taught her how to write, when she used to go to Carnish School.'

Margaret opened her handbag and began to rummage through its contents.

'What are you raking for in that bag of yours, girl?' Kirsty said. 'Are you looking for your autogram book?'

'Paracetamol,' Margaret said. 'Ah, here they are.' She snapped off the lid of the container and gulped and gasped as she tried to choke down a number of tablets.

'Well,' Kirsty said, 'are you two going to sit around here all day like members of a jury in Lochmaddy court? That's it. Clear out of my sight. I'll not put my name to paper for anybody but Tiny. You'd better go before Miss Maclean comes back.'

'Come on, Jean,' Margaret said, 'I haven't the foggiest notion what she's on about.'

'There you go, Kirsty, dear,' Jean said, and she gave Kirsty a violent, wet kiss. 'It saddens me to be leaving you, parting is so painful . . .' She burst into floods of tears. 'I'm utterly dejected . . .'

'That's enough, Jean,' Margaret said. 'You're making me irritable.'

'What else is new?' Jean said.

'Stop this quarrelling,' Kirsty said. 'Miss Maclean doesn't like squabbling in school.'

'We'll be seeing you, Kirsty,' Margaret said. 'I'll tell Tiny you were asking for him, when I see him.' She lowered her voice to a mere whisper. 'And certainly I've a feeling I'll be paying him a visit very soon.'

They left and in less than a minute they were outside the nursing home.

'You know what, Margaret?' Jean said. 'I enjoyed my trip very much.'

'Well,' Margaret said, 'I didn't.'

'That place isn't bad at all,' Jean said. 'If I had said to you ten years ago, "Hey, how would you fancy, girl, taking a run to Carnish for a chat with the old folks?" you'd have thought I was cracked. How times have changed, eh?'

'No, Jean,' Margaret said, 'they haven't. I've always thought you were cracked. And I still do.'

8

Davy enjoys the good life

There is a depleted quarry, halfway between Daliburgh and Frobost, in South Uist. In the darkness Duncan MacCormack drove the Lexus carefully inside, lights on high beam. He stopped the car beside a caravan that had been painted yellow. The windows of the trailer were curtained. He saw light glowing behind them.

Duncan shut off the lights and the engine. He walked stiffly to the door of the caravan and knocked four times. On the edge of his vision he noticed a motorbike parked at the far end of the trailer.

Davy opened the door and chuckled. 'Duncan, my very good friend, come on in.'

Duncan followed him inside and found himself in a very cosy, compact living space.

Davy opened two cans of beer and gave one to Duncan.

'Cheers, Davy,' Duncan said. 'I really like the place . . . the, umh, "Camper" you've got for yourself.'

'Modified Winnebago,' Davy said. 'Modified Winnebago is the name of this rig. I'm leasing it.'

'Excuse me,' Duncan said. 'It's nice. And you're

looking better too. Love the baggy combats, and the sports top. CK?'

'Calvin Klein,' Davy said, a hint of pride in his voice.

'Poor people's clothing,' Duncan said. 'Very popular gear that is . . . in the South Bronx and . . . in Possil-park. I see you've got yourself a motorbike too.'

'Suzuki Bandit,' Davy said. 'Five fifty from a tink in Inversneckie. Goes well, though.'

'Things're goin' a little bit better,' Duncan said.

'Things're a lot better,' Davy said. 'I was out last night, me and this girl, and I had a place to go to and wheels to take her to the place. It's really neat.'

'You look a lot happier,' Duncan said, 'and that's good.'

'Certainly is,' Davy said.

'You don't look like somebody's just run over your dog with a tractor,' Duncan said. 'So whose land are we on just now?'

'Who the hell knows?' Davy said. 'Some teacher in Glasgow or somewhere like that. He's left the tenancy of the croft – you can see the old ruin outside in daylight – when his grandfather's brother dies, and he won't come back home until he retires and, in the meantime, I'm the sub-tenant. Those folk at the Crofters' Commission couldn't care less.'

'They're pretty sloppy right enough,' Duncan said. 'I can vouch for that myself.'

'That's right,' Davy said. 'I always wondered how you got that croft in North Uist . . . where the Russian girls . . . where my wife . . . Tamara – the bitch – does all that aromatherapy stuff . . . if that's what you call it.'

'Don't worry about it,' Duncan said. 'What are you up to, Davy?'

'Well,' Davy said, 'I was goin' to talk to you about that, if you came down, you know?'

'The house in Strumore's terribly busy,' Duncan said.

'Some woman or other . . . the Factor's daughter in North Uist . . . has been pretty busy too, I'm hearing,' Davy said.

'She's into "aromatherapy" too?' Duncan said.

'No,' Davy said, 'she's a lawyer in Edinburgh. But her father's not keeping well, it seems, so she's been helping her mother at home. She's been visiting this old woman in Trianaid pretty often, asking her questions and writing down everything she says.'

'Maybe she's making a documentary for television,' Duncan said. 'You know, one of these boring programmes we get all the time? *Looking Back* or *Bygone Days* . . . that kind of rubbish.'

'I don't think that's what she's doin',' Davy said. 'She's not a foreigner. She's got plenty Gaelic.'

Duncan burst out laughing. 'Did you hear about the programme that's coming out this winter? *Let's Go Back*? Starts at two o'clock in the morning, finishes at half past one.'

'I'm just telling you what I've heard,' Davy said. 'We don't have to be worried about this woman, do we?'

'No, indeed,' Duncan said, 'the only thing that concerns me is the major companies that are actively pursuing me.'

'What companies?' Davy said.

'MasterCard, Visa, American Express,' Duncan said.

'Oh . . . I see,' Davy said. 'This is debts you had, is it?'

'Och, I paid them off a long time ago,' Duncan said. 'They're in a frenzy to offer me credit.'

'Lucky you!' Davy said. 'That's the thing I wanted to talk to you about, you come down, you know?'

'What thing?' Duncan said.

'I was wondering,' Davy said, 'you got anything else in mind?'

'Jesus, Davy, I don't know,' Duncan said. 'You fancy getting married again, eh? What a stud you are!'

'Me and that big, ugly freak aren't married,' Davy said. 'I was thinking, the reason everything went so smooth and clean the last time was that you're really terrific at setting things up.'

'Something's been festering at the back of my mind right enough,' Duncan said.

'I'm up for anything,' Davy said.

'Are you any good at impersonating folk?' Duncan said. 'Well, women in particular?'

'You know this, Duncan?' Davy said. 'One fine day I'm going to break your jaw for you.'

'Take it easy, boy,' Duncan said. 'You don't have to be all dressed up like a woman . . . though it might help if you were in full drag . . . what I'm looking for is somebody who can speak in a woman's voice.'

Davy spoke in a soft falsetto. 'You want me to talk like this?'

'Well,' Duncan said, 'maybe with a little training . . . some half-wit might think you were female. That is, if he'd just spent ten years in St Kilda. Doesn't matter. You'd be on the phone anyway.'

'I'm to be chirping on the phone?' Davy said. 'Who am I goin' to be talking to?'

'People are obsessed by youth nowadays,' Duncan said. 'Know who're being ignored?'

'No,' Davy said.

'Old men,' Duncan said.

'Old men?' Davy said.

'Old men still like to be titillated by women,' Duncan said. 'It's just that they don't get the chance any more. We should have fun chat-lines for old men.'

'And, if some dirty old man phones up frothing at the mouth,' Davy said, gulping his words, 'I've got to chat to him?'

'Both of you would be doing it,' Duncan said. 'Deer-hunter able to do a woman's voice?'

'I never asked him, to tell the truth,' Davy said. 'That was never a question that ever came up between us. But anyway, Calum's off. Him and the North Uist boy he's killing stags with. When he gets his money in Germany he's goin' to buy . . . gear in Amsterdam.'

'He'll make a fortune off of that,' Duncan said.

'Maybe he will,' Davy said, 'and maybe they'll grab him as soon as he starts to sell the stuff in the pubs around Uist. He'll have more people watching him than Huw Edwards. That's a very dangerous trade. Think I still prefer the phone. I don't have to talk dirty, do I?'

'No, of course not, my friend,' Duncan said. 'You'll have a script. All you have to do is read it . . . in a woman's voice.'

'That's easy enough for you to say,' Davy said. 'What if I've got a script and the old man has a different script?'

'You've got to trick them,' Duncan said. 'While the pair of you are talking, you keep control of the conversation. Like, the old man will have a feeble, croaky voice. Like this: "Who's this? Is this Conversation Without Bounds?"' Duncan pitched his voice much higher. '"Yes, it is, love," the woman will say.' Duncan reverted to the old man's voice. '"Well, I'm sitting crouched over the fire, and I haven't got a soul to talk to."' Duncan did his female voice. '"Do you want me to come over? I'll hold your hand." The old guy will get excited. "Oh, God! Yes!"' Duncan assumed the woman's voice again. '"Then, I'm going to take your jersey and tuck it round your shoulders so you don't get a draught." The old guy will get very excited. "Oh, God! Yes, yes!"' Duncan imitated the woman. '"And then, I'm going to talk to you about the Second World War, the whaling in South Georgia and how the *Politician* went aground on Eriskay." At this point the old man is absolutely ecstatic. "God have mercy! Keep going, keep going. Don't stop."' Duncan spoke in his normal voice. 'It'll be easy money for you, Davy.'

'This is starting to appeal to me, Duncan,' Davy said.

'Mind you, you won't get the money in one big lump sum this time,' Duncan said. 'You'll be paid according to the hours you work, you understand?'

'Just as long as the odd bit of change is coming in regularly,' Davy said. 'It's funny this kind of thing. Like the last thing we did, you can tell right off you're goin' to get a result. I had a good feeling about Dearest Dacha and I've a good feeling about this.'

9

Watch it, MacAskill!

'He's a fool,' Margaret said. 'He's cunning all right, but he's still a fool.' She and MacAskill were seated inside the Land-Rover on a wet, stormy night outside Clachan na Luib Church, in North Uist.

'I'm pretty devious myself at times,' MacAskill said. 'You can't be straight with people all the time.'

'Oh, I know, Mr MacAskill,' Margaret said. 'And so will your wife Mary know if you don't keep your hands on the steering wheel.'

'My hands are on the steering wheel,' MacAskill said.

'Keep them there,' Margaret said. 'There's a good boy. You're learning. Now, Tiny, he doesn't learn at all. You could tell him till you're blue in the face why he shouldn't do something, he doesn't listen to a word anybody says, and he goes right ahead and does it anyway.'

'Well,' MacAskill said, 'we don't all stick to the straight and narrow all the time, know what I mean?'

'I play it straight,' Margaret said, 'and so will you, just as long as you're with me. But Duncan MacCormack, he's not like that. He pulls some stroke or other and people find out about it. Instead of being ashamed he's got the cheek to try a new trick the following day. Other guys, after doing something naughty, they lie low for a while until things have cooled down a bit. You know the Elder?'

'No,' MacAskill said, 'I don't think I've heard of anybody that goes by the name of the Elder.'

'The Elder is a fine man,' Margaret said. 'He's a guy I know. A real kind gentleman from Lewis. Does some work for me occasionally when I need somebody who looks really wild and tough – say, I've sent out a bill and some hero decides he's not going to pay, you understand?'

'I'm afraid I do,' MacAskill said.

'Well, the wife gets a call from the Elder at the house. The Elder puts the fear of death into her. You'd think to hear him talking he had something seriously wrong with his throat. "Where is he? I call him at the office, he's not in. Same thing at the house. He lives in a tent, is that it? Ask him to call me," he says. Always, they call. After they talk to the Elder they understand they've got to pay me. Takes some time, but gradually they get used to the idea it's inevitable, and I get a cheque.'

'You want to hire this Elder fellow, do you?' Mac-Askill said.

'Maybe,' Margaret said. 'Aside from Tiny, there's two other guys involved in this. There's one young guy from Boisdale who does things for Duncan Mac-Cormack and who went on an expedition to Ireland with him. That one I'm fairly sure of. The other kid, I'm

41

not so sure about. He's disappeared somewhere. But he is a Macdonald.'

'That the fellow who's married to one of the Russian girls?' MacAskill said.

'They've both got Russian wives,' Margaret said. 'The first kid – he's called Davy – he's married to Tamara, the big weight-lifter, but I don't think he sees much of her after what happened at the Registry Office.'

'What happened?' MacAskill said.

'Some kind of mishap,' Margaret said. 'Don't ask. He freaked out. No wonder. That woman knows tricks. And if your Mary knew about them, she'd go down to the police station and ask them to arrest her.'

'Hmmm,' MacAskill said, 'things are going to hell on wheels. Himself is not terribly pleased at all.'

'I can believe it,' Margaret said.

'As you know,' MacAskill said, 'Queen Elizabeth – she and Lord Granville are cousins – is coming to Vallay next month, and it seems she's not going to allow Philip to come with her. "How the good folk of Uist have deteriorated!" she told Lord Granville on the phone the night before last. The affair has got really serious.'

'It must have done,' Margaret said, 'if the royal family says so. They've got a lot of experience of really serious stuff.'

'I'm not joking,' MacAskill said.

'Save us, of course you're not,' Margaret said.

'We've got to get rid of the girls,' MacAskill said.

'That can be done,' Margaret said.

'What about this Tiny fellow?' MacAskill said. 'He's the worst of the lot in my opinion.'

'You're not wrong,' Margaret said. 'Compared to Duncan MacCormack, Rob Roy MacGregor was just a barefoot boy. Think about it, he conned poor old Kirsty. But we'll not confront him just yet. Wait'll we get shot of the girls. It'll make him easier. But, sure, we'll do it.'

'How are you going to tackle them?' MacAskill said.

'Maybe I'll have to give a bell to Stornoway,' Margaret said. 'I'll phone my good friend, the Elder.'

'Lord Granville doesn't want a war to break out on account of this,' MacAskill said.

'I'm sure he doesn't,' Margaret said. 'Mr MacAskill, you go and talk to Lord Granville. Tell him we've got to chase the Russians – and the ostriches – out of North Uist. He'll agree with you.'

'So, we leave the lads alone just now?' MacAskill said.

'Let's just think about the girls for now,' Margaret said. 'The Elder will sort them out. He's been at this game a long time. He's one of the best.'

'But, you're able to do all this, though?' MacAskill said.

'For the right price,' Margaret said, 'anyone can do almost anything.' She paused for a moment. 'Oh, that reminds me of something.'

'What?' MacAskill said.

'I'll need to get a loan from you,' Margaret said.

'What do you need?' MacAskill said.

'Listen,' Margaret said, 'you and me are getting well acquainted here, right?'

'Yes,' MacAskill said, a broad grin on his face.

'Give me the Land-Rover for two or three days,' Margaret said.

The man from Harris frowned. 'But . . . but . . .'

'Out you get,' Margaret said.

MacAskill opened his mouth as if to speak but no sound emerged. He opened the door and got out. He started to walk in the direction of Lochmaddy. Rain poured down heavily in a stormy wind.

10

The deed you do in the back will come to the front door

'How much sugar do you take, Calum?' Davy said. On a cold morning, Davy was busy in the kitchen, which was situated next to the door of his caravan. Morag Macdonald murmured softly from a radio on the worktop next to the sink. Calum was singing in the shower-stall at the far end of the living space.

'Two and a half,' Calum said, his voice muffled by the sound of water.

The shower was turned off. The shower curtain parted.

'Your breakfast is on the table,' Davy said. 'I think I'll tidy up these cases of yours.' He went over to the centre of the room where a pile of suitcases and bags lay in disarray and began to put them in order. One bag that had not been closed properly fell to the floor with a thud.

'Oh, God have mercy!' Davy gasped. 'Where did all these packages come from?' He quickly lifted scores of packets, all wrapped in brown paper and weighing half an ounce, and crammed them into the bag.

Calum rushed towards Davy and roared at the top of

his voice. 'From J.D. Williams, you fuckin' half-wit!' He crashed into Davy and the pair of them started to wrestle on the floor. When he got Davy on his back and subdued the lad, he hissed with anger. 'Things . . . that don't belong to you . . . keep your hands off them.'

'I was just trying to help you, man,' Davy said.

'I've a good mind to give you a punch,' Calum said, 'that'd floor you for good.' He got up, took hold of the boy's arm and dragged him to his feet.

'Why are you so angry?' Davy said. 'I know fine what's in them. I've no time for that stuff . . . hey, Calum?'

'What?' Calum said.

'Aren't you goin' to put some clothes on, man?' Davy said.

'I've got nothing to hide,' Calum said, smiling at the old joke. He quickly put on a pair of trousers. 'Umh, who told you about my secret stash?'

'Nobody!' Davy said. 'You guys were in Amsterdam!'

'You're lying!' Calum said. He smiled the universal minimal smile, lips parted showing only part of his teeth. 'You've been talking to Tommy. What did he say?'

'He never said a word to me,' Davy said. 'I don't even know the boy. A prick like that from North Uist. I don't trust these people. They're two-faced and they're so holy, by their way of it.'

'Maybe you're not telling lies,' Calum said. 'I don't know. I'm absolutely knackered after that journey.'

'How did the pair of you get on?' Davy said.

'Went like a good Gaelic song,' Calum said. 'We left

on the first ferry Tuesday morning, took turns driving down to Newcastle. We slept aboard Tuesday night and we arrived in Holland late Wednesday.'

'That kind of driving'll take it out of you,' Davy said.

'Och,' Calum said, 'it wasn't the driving that wore me out, but Tommy's non-stop gibbering about computers and gigabytes. And the smell.'

'Tommy smells?' Davy said.

'He might have been as pure as a mountain stream when we left,' Calum said, 'but I'm telling you there was a stink off him that'd fell a pig before we got to Hamburg. You ever been locked up in a Morris Minor van with half a ton of meat that's fast goin' off in the back?'

'No,' Davy said, 'but I've been in the public bar in Creagorry before going to the dance in Balivanich on games day.'

'You're only a soft potato,' Calum said. He took a sip of coffee. 'Round about Bremen we're in a rainstorm. I thought I saw rain in Uist, but, Christ, this was a downpour and a half. We couldn't leave the windows down in case we drowned and when they were up we nearly suffocated. It was hellish.'

'But you met up with the Germans eventually?' Davy said.

'We did indeed,' Calum said. 'Sold the venison for a good price and . . .'

'What did you get for it?' Davy said.

'Mind your own business,' Calum said. 'I got plenty. And in our own currency too.'

'What difference did that make?' Davy said.

'Davy, Davy,' Calum said, 'what am I going to do with you? Don't you know anything about the exchange rate? How clued up are you about the metric system?'

'Tell you the truth,' Davy said, 'I wouldn't know a kilo from the leg of a cow.'

'That's what I thought,' Calum said. 'Look, the value of our currency goes up and down. When the pound is high, we say that it's up. When it's low compared to the Deutschmark or the Euro, we say it's down. Up and down, strong or weak . . . it's just physics.'

'Physics?' Davy said. 'When did you study physics? A guy who was kept back so often in school that you couldn't go to Primary Four without having a shave in the morning?'

'I'll bet you too,' Calum said, 'you don't know the difference between a metric ounce and an ounce in this country.'

'I don't, and I'm not really bothered,' Davy said, 'but I've a feeling you're goin' to tell me anyway.'

'Say you're in Amsterdam,' Calum said, 'and you're goin' to buy . . . umh, stuff. These Dutch guys come up to you and they've got a kind of menu. Nepalese at five pounds a gramme; Afghan Black three pounds a gramme; Moroccan two pounds fifty . . . and so on. Seven metric grammes, that's a quarter ounce by our Imperial measure. That means there's twenty-eight grammes to the ounce by our measurements, but according to the metric system – and that's the system the Dutch use – there's only twenty-five grammes to the ounce. So, when you buy a nine-ounce bar – a 'Nine-Bar' they call it – you've got to be careful that you're not an ounce short. Get it?'

'You've got my head leaking, Calum,' Davy said. 'By the way, how many Nine-Bars did you buy?'

'Eight,' Calum said. 'Nepalese. For two thousand pounds.'

'And what'll you get for them?' Davy said.

'If I sell them as half quarters,' Calum said, 'I'll get twenty pounds for each bit. Count it all up yourself.'

'I don't think I can do that,' Davy said.

'It's easy,' Calum said. 'Forty pounds for every quarter ounce. A hundred and sixty for an ounce. One thousand, four hundred and forty pounds for every Nine-Bar.'

'And you've got eight of those,' Davy said. He inhaled. 'Do you know what? I hate drugs with a vengeance, Calum. I don't want to hear any more about them. It's early, but I need a dram.' He walked over to a cabinet and took out a bottle. 'What do you think of this? Glenfarclas, eh? Have I come up in the world or what?'

'Physics, boy,' Calum said.

'What do you mean, physics?' Davy said. 'Don't start your lecturing again.'

Calum lowered his voice. 'The first law in physics: what goes up must come down.'

'What?' Davy said.

Calum said, 'You think we did terribly well out of that marriage ceremony, don't you?'

'Yeah. Tiny set it up for us and we got a result.'

'Always do what *Tiny* says,' Calum said in sarcastic tones, 'and you'll never go far wrong.' He chewed on a piece of bacon and took a mouthful of coffee. He belched. 'To the hospital, perhaps, but never far wrong.'

Davy swallowed a piece of white pudding and said, 'It worked out beautiful.' 'That what you think?' Calum said. 'Of course, they're now after us, but it worked out beautiful. Me and you, boy, we've got different ideas of beautiful.'

'What the fuck do you mean?' Davy said.

'You, me and Tiny,' Calum said. 'They know all about us and somebody's goin' to pay us a visit soon. And he's goin' to have a shinty stick with him. I hang around here too long – which I'm not goin' to do – they'll break my kneecaps for me and I'm goin' to be as busted up as you guys are. I'm making for Germany. I know people over there and we'll get something going together.'

'Why do you have to run?'

'Cut your gibbering, Davy,' Calum said. Two seconds passed. 'For Dearest Dacha. The fuck's the matter with you?'

'What the fuck's the matter with you? Where did this crazy story come from, anyway. You been testing the Nepalese?'

'Davy,' Calum said quietly, 'the Elder is coming.'

'The Elder?' Davy said, a quiver in his voice. 'God preserve us! Who told you this?'

'Tommy.'

'Calum, this is Tommy Matheson we're talking about, right?'

50

'Right, Tommy was telling me.' Calum sighed. 'We're talking, there's a stink in the van and it's raining and the journey's taking so long and everything, and he tells me that his aunt, the daughter of the Factor in North Uist, has sent word to Stornoway to bring this monster person down.'

'How did he know this?' Davy said.

'He was the one who sent the e-mail. He can navigate that internet as well as his old man can make his way to the pub in Carnish. He said that this Margaret woman asked him to send the letter, that two Russian girls were dispensing hospitality to men . . . and rearing ostriches . . . in Strumore and that the Elder would have to teach them a lesson.'

Davy gazed at Calum with eyes that were fearful and sad. 'I heard the ostriches died.'

'I heard an old fellow from Kyles Flodda died over there too,' Calum said. 'Heart failure or something.'

Davy began to move his head around, first to the left, then to the right. 'Never mind that. And what did you say, in case the Elder doesn't know where we all live when he comes visiting?'

'I never opened my mouth,' Calum said. There was a brief pause. 'Well, maybe I mentioned the wedding down in Glasgow. It was hilarious when you fainted and Tamara had to lift you up.' He stopped talking for an instant. 'And we spoke for a while about Tiny. Tommy was the one who put all the circuits into the house in Strumore, and he hasn't had his wages yet from Duncan. Never mind, young man, I never mentioned

51

you. I didn't say anything else. All I could think about was getting home to sell the stuff and getting out of here.'

'Thanks, Calum,' Davy said. 'I've got to give you credit, boy. You don't bullshit a man. With you, it's the truth that matters. Your friends are in danger and you don't say, "Jesus, Davy, the Elder is goin' to bust our kneecaps. We'll stick together and get him first." You say you're goin' to get out and to me you say "fuck you". With you, a man knows he's got to stand alone. Until the kneecaps go, anyway.'

'I better go,' said Calum. 'I've got a lot to do before I get that plane.'

'Duncan'll be raging mad when he finds out about this,' Davy said.

'He's allowed,' Calum said. 'What if Tiny gets raging mad? I couldn't care less. What can he do to me? Oh, he'll maybe not let me see *Postman Pat* on telly. Fuck him.'

11

Fear is worse than war

Davy MacIsaac drove the Suzuki into the courtyard of the Polochar Inn, South Uist. He stopped, shut off the ignition and dismounted. He put the motorbike in an upright position. He walked towards the door with his hands clasped tightly to his chest to prevent them shaking. This was his posture when he sat down at a table where Duncan sat with a glass of whisky in front of him.

'Is this you saying your prayers, Davy?' Duncan said to the lad.

'A lot of good that would do me,' Davy said. 'Calum's betrayed us.'

'How?' Duncan said.

'He's spilled his guts about Dearest Dacha, the carry-on Tanya and Tamara have been having and . . . the ostriches. The Factor's daughter in North Uist has sent word to Stornoway to a guy called the Elder. He'll be coming here soon and he's going to get rid of the Russians and he's goin' to break my kneecaps. He'll do the same to Calum if he gets hold of him.'

'You sure, Davy?'

Davy spoke earnestly. 'As sure as I'm alive . . . however long that'll be.'

'Well, you're the one who wanted him along with you,' Duncan said. 'You said he'd be all right. Remember that?'

'You're a right bastard,' Davy said.

'I doubt it,' Duncan said. 'I've seen my old man, and he looks a lot like me.'

'I made a mistake,' Davy said. 'How the fuck'd I know Calum was goin' to be like this? I didn't know he was goin' to make his confession to a black Protestant – a guy who's related to the Factor in North Uist.'

'You'd have to have eyes at the back of your head before you'd be up to the carry-on of some wives,' Duncan said. 'You're in the hole right enough, kid. You used to slag me off quite a bit about the "Death Before The Free Church" T-shirts. It was me that picked those words. I was guilty of that.'

'You made a mistake that time,' Davy said. 'This time round, I've got to do something myself. If I'm in the shit, he's the one that put me there, and I could kill him for it, I really could.'

'I don't think you should do that,' Duncan said. 'Let the Elder deal with him.'

'Then the mad bastard comes after me?' Davy said. 'Course, they're not your kneecaps, but that doesn't matter, does it?'

'Anyway,' Duncan said, 'there's no way I'm tied to these Russian girls. I didn't get married down in Glasgow.' He closed his mouth and frowned. 'Of course there's always the house in Strumore, but I'm not responsible for the behaviour of the people who live in it. And this is the proof.'

'Don't kid yourself, Duncan,' Davy said. 'You're in danger too. Forget Calum for the minute. Either he'll go to Germany or the Elder will grab him before he does.' He smirked briefly. 'Or, he'll get caught by the police with that stuff on him, and he'll go to prison.'

'We've got to concentrate on the Elder. Don't open your door to anyone with a Lewis accent . . . you hear somebody cackling like a hen outside get out as quick as you can.'

'No, that's not how I see things,' Duncan said. 'I don't think even the Elder could beat Tamara and Tanya if it came to fisticuffs. As for you, although the pair of you are married, you're kind of separated and she's doin' her own thing.'

'Duncan, I hope you're right,' Davy said. 'I'm really attached to these kneecaps of mine. I'd like to keep them for a long time yet.'

'I'm right,' Duncan said.

'You don't mind, though,' Davy said, 'if I go and stay for a while with Alina and the kids . . . and the Lego pieces?'

'Davy,' Duncan said, 'you can go and stay with your wife in Strumore, if it'd make you feel safer with her protecting you. We'll get out of this. I'm going to write a couple of scripts for the old boys. You'll get word from me when it's time to stop worrying and start working again.'

12

A goat's eyes in the head of the Elder

Murdo MacIver, also known as the Elder, was immense. His torso was so broad and thick that it was a wonder his legs, themselves like muscled columns, could support it. In the cafeteria at Balivanich airport in Benbecula, he walked slowly towards the table where Margaret was sitting. His face was a soft one, his small brown eyes like sleepy raisins.

'Margaret,' the Elder said. He had a high-pitched, reedy voice, which a lot of men who fight acquire through being punched in the throat.

'Murdo,' Margaret said. 'Coffee?'

'No,' the Elder said. 'Any chance of getting a proper drink?'

'It's only half past ten,' Margaret said. 'I don't know if the bar's open yet.'

'What'll you have?' the young waitress, a blonde teenager, enquired.

'Just a couple of bottles of beer,' Margaret said.

'Uh uh,' the Elder said.

'What do you want?' Margaret said.

'Dark rum – a large,' the Elder said.

'I don't think we're selling spirits just now,' the young girl said. 'I'll do my best.'

'You do that, darling,' the Elder said, 'and maybe I'll give you my phone number.'

'Murdo!' Margaret said. 'That lassie's still at school.'

'All the better,' the Elder said. 'Train them when they're young, that's the best thing for them.'

'You got a glow on, Murdo?' Margaret said.

'I had a dram on the plane,' the Elder said.

'Maybe more than one?' Margaret said.

'Well,' the Elder said, 'maybe I had two or three.'

'You eaten yet?' Margaret said.

'On the plane,' the Elder said. 'I didn't eat any of the stuff they gave us. The meat was so undercooked, you could almost hear it barking when you took a bite of it. I had a chocolate biscuit.'

'You ought to have a roll here,' Margaret said.

'Not hungry,' the Elder said. He turned his head towards the serving counter. 'Where did that retard of a girl go?' He noticed the girl approaching with their drinks. 'Hey, get a move on, I'm as dry as a cork over here.'

'There you go,' the young blonde said. 'Angus wasn't all that keen on opening the bar at first but he made an exception eventually.'

'Where do you have to go to talk to Angus?' the Elder said.

The waitress did not reply.

'I asked you,' the Elder said quietly, 'where do you have to go to talk to good old Angus. I know it's outside

57

the building here. You maybe had to jump on your micro scooter, or take a bus. I was just wondering.'

'Angus is the boss,' the young girl said.

'Murdo, leave her alone,' Margaret said.

The Elder raised the glass and drained it in one gulp. 'Another large one for me, and do you want anything, Margaret?'

'No,' Margaret said, 'I'm fine.' She crouched down as though looking for her handbag and whispered under her breath, 'But I don't think you are.'

'That really gets on my nerves,' the Elder said. 'Young things with big tits and everything, they won't do a hand's turn unless you're watching them. They're . . . they don't give a shit for people who're waiting for some service. All they can think about is boyfriends.'

'She did you a favour,' Margaret said.

'Aye,' the Elder said, 'she ran to Creagorry to get a dram for me.'

'You never used to be so keen on the booze,' Margaret said. 'You still taking communion?'

'No,' the Elder said, 'I had to give that up. The other elders withheld the communion from me. I was summoned before the Back elders – the most powerful group in the Western Isles.'

'What put them against you?' Margaret said.

'There was this young girl,' the Elder said, 'and she was kind of religious . . . and I used to help her with the Shorter Catechism and stuff like that. You know what they did? Oh, they're a horrible lot. Know what the folk in Back say?'

'No,' Margaret said.

'They have a motto,' the Elder said. ' "We don't eat our young here in Back. We eat *your* young." They were spying on us while we were parked in the car outside the house of Alex the Grass. Right enough, it was kind of late, and she had school to go to in the morning but . . . it wasn't fair what the deacon said to me at the full session. "Hand over your soft hat, Murdo. The great church of Back is no place for the likes of you." I'm on the dole and I'm on Big Kenny's programme now and again.'

'Gosh,' Margaret said, 'I wouldn't think you'd make much at that.'

'I don't get a penny,' the Elder said. ' "Thanks a lot" if I'm lucky. But I'll find something.'

'Well,' Margaret said, 'I've got something for you here.'

'Thank the Lord God,' the Elder said. 'I'm really hurting for the money just now. It's hard getting work like this nowadays. People have been staying away from me lately.'

'You don't say?' Margaret said.

'You don't mind,' the Elder said, 'if I drink a mouthful of your beer while I'm waiting for that ugly bitch to make it back from Lochboisdale?' He did not wait for permission and drank half the contents of her glass.

'God,' Margaret said, 'what a thirst you've got, man!'

'I was up all night,' the Elder said. 'I never sleep a wink, I'm goin' on the plane the next day. Planes make me nervous. We finish here I'm heading straight for the bed as soon as we get to the hotel.'

'How're Peggy and the kids?' Margaret said.

'Hellish,' the Elder said. 'Donald's turned into a waster. He left school last spring and all he does is smoke that stuff. Kylie's got a boyfriend. She's fourteen years old and she's on the pill.'

'No kidding!' Margaret said.

'You just can't believe it,' the Elder said. 'I said to Peggy, "In the name of God, will you tell me, what's goin' on in this house?" She says, "You want, you'd probably prefer she gets pregnant." I couldn't believe it. "Peggy," I said, "she's fourteen years old. She's started a bit early, do you not think?"'

'I think so, too,' Margaret said.

The young waitress arrived and placed a glass of rum on the table. 'Dark rum – double,' she said.

'Bet you didn't bring her a beer,' the Elder said.

'No,' the girl said politely, 'you only wanted the rum, I thought.'

'You thought wrong,' the Elder said. 'Go and get her a bottle of beer. I've drunk her beer on her.'

'I don't want any more, Murdo,' Margaret said. 'It's all right.'

'Bring her a beer,' the Elder said. He drank a mouthful of rum. 'Yeah, Kylie's too young.'

'I agree with you,' Margaret said.

'You know what Peggy says to me?' the Elder said. 'She says, "How old was Natalie when you were goin' with her?"'

'How old was Natalie?' Margaret said.

'Sixteen,' the Elder said, 'which is a completely different thing.'

'I believe you, Murdo,' Margaret said.

'Everything goes to hell if you wait long enough,' the Elder said. He stopped talking, as if he had just remembered something. 'And Peggy's got herself a toy-boy. I know who he is and everything, but that stuff leaves you so tired I can't be bothered getting up and doing something about it.'

'God save us,' Margaret said.

The waitress arrived and thumped the bottle on the table.

'Congratulations, dear,' the Elder said, 'you managed, finally. Traffic was bad, I suppose.'

'You're not having any more,' Margaret said. 'You're goin' to collapse.'

The Elder began to drink, rum and beer, alternatively. 'I've got a great capacity for drink. So, what're we doin'?'

'We've got two Russian girls and a couple of lads,' Margaret said. 'Well, there's really three guys, but one of them's missing just now and I thought I'd get rid of a couple. That'd leave the girls and Duncan MacCormack for you to do.' She looked up as the young girl appeared with a bill in her hand. 'What do I owe you, miss?' she said. She took out a purse and MasterCard and extended the card to the girl.

'On your way back,' the Elder said, 'if you think you're goin' to be in the neighbourhood again this year, you can bring me another one.'

'You can't, miss,' Margaret said. 'I'm going to drink this, even if I don't want it. He's drinking coffee. Give the man a black coffee.'

'Hey,' the Elder said, 'take it easy.'

'Hey,' Margaret said, 'you take it easy. Coffee for you, boy.'

'I won't be able to sleep,' the Elder said, 'if I take coffee.'

'Read the Shorter Catechism,' Margaret said.

'I don't think I'll be doing that,' the Elder said. 'You're going to fix me up with a lump of that stuff.'

'You need that as well?' Margaret said.

'Relax, I'm not working tonight, am I?' the Elder said.

'No,' Margaret said.

'I'm probably not goin' to be working tomorrow night, either,' the Elder said. 'What day is it today, anyway?'

'Tuesday,' Margaret said.

'I don't like doin' things as fast as this,' the Elder said. 'This is Tuesday, I'll go and talk to the Russians on Sunday night. That's when I'm goin' to scare the shit out of them. You people in Uist are so impatient. You don't take time to think about things. I do.'

'It's always good to meet a man I can learn something from,' Margaret said.

'I've been at this game a long time,' the Elder said. 'That leaves me free for five nights, then. Who's coming to the hotel with the stuff tonight?'

'I don't know,' Margaret said. 'I'll do my best. Someone'll come.'

13

A visit to the house of the ostriches

When Margaret and her nephew, Tommy Matheson, arrived at Dearest Dacha in Strumore in their Land-Rover they stopped and gazed at Tanya who was outside feeding the ostriches.

'God, what a size she is!' Tommy, a handsome, fair-haired lad of nineteen, exclaimed.

'That one who's feeding the ostriches just now, that's Tanya,' Margaret said. 'Wait till you see the other one.'

'The other one's bigger than Tanya?' Tommy said.

'A lot bigger,' Margaret said.

'God save me,' Tommy said. 'You see her at the disco you'd go, "That's goin' to take a lot of trips to the toilet with the half-bottle." '

'Aren't you lucky!' Margaret said. 'You're goin' to get to meet them and you won't need a half-bottle at all.'

'What're we goin' to do, Margaret?' Tommy said.

'You're goin' to sit down,' Margaret said, 'and you're goin' to pout so as to look sexy.'

'What're you goin' to be doin'?' Tommy said.

'Never mind thinking about what I'm goin' to do,'

Margaret said. 'You just think about what you're goin' to do. Try and smile a lot, too.'

'Do I get some money?' Tommy said.

'Two hundred,' Margaret said, 'and you'll get a car out of it too.'

'What kind?' Tommy said.

'Land-Rover,' Margaret said. 'This one.'

'But that's MacAskill's car,' Tommy said. 'It belongs to the estate.'

'It's yours now,' Margaret said.

'Okay,' Tommy said, 'but why're you bein' so generous? You're making me think.'

'That's your weak spot, Thomas,' Margaret said. 'Don't you be thinking at all. Just do as I tell you, and you've got nothing to worry about.'

'God, here she comes,' Tommy said.

'Greetings, comrades,' Tanya bawled. 'You want to enter Dacha? Show not begin until twenty-three hundred hours, but mother and son welcome to have glass of wodka.'

'She thinks you're my mother,' Tommy said, laughing.

'Thank you' Margaret said. 'We follow you.'

'Come,' Tanya said, 'you meet my friend Tamara.'

The front door squeaked as Tanya opened it. The three of them entered.

Tamara, dressed in shorts and singlet, stood in the middle of the room. She was exercising with a large ball and dripping sweat. Tanya and Tamara spoke in their own language for a while. Then Tamara broke off her conversation and turned to Margaret. 'Wodka for you?'

'Yes, please,' Tommy said.

'Tommy!' Margaret said. 'No, thank you. I want to talk to you both . . . Me, Tanya and Tamara . . . We talk, okay?'

'Okay,' Tamara said.

'You like working in Scotland?' Margaret said.

'Is okay,' Tamara said.

'Better in Germany, no?' Margaret said. 'Many roubles there.'

Tamara replied with enthusiasm, 'Yes, yes, yes!'

'You like to go work in Germany?' Margaret said, running her tongue over her lips.

The pair of them displayed great excitement. '*Da*, *da*, *da*!' they exclaimed together.

'You like to go with . . . him?' Margaret said.

'*Da*, *da*, *da*!' they said.

'Hold on a minute, Margaret,' Tommy said, 'I don't like . . .'

'What did I tell you?' Margaret said. 'Shut up.'

'How old your son?' Tamara said.

'Nineteen,' Margaret said.

'Younger than husband of Tamara, Dah-vee,' Tanya said. 'What his name?

'Tommy,' Margaret said.

'To-mee is pretty boy, no?' Tamara said.

There followed a machine-gun exchange in Russian.

'What's that dopey bitch saying?' Tommy said.

'They think you're not bad-looking at all,' Margaret said. 'I think Tanya's fallen for you.'

'God preserve me!' Tommy said, a hint of anxiety in his voice.

'You go to Germany with Tommy?' Margaret said. 'He has a good car and knows the way to Hamburg.'

Tanya and Tamara spoke in unison. '*Da*, *da*, *da*! Hamburg is good! To-mee is good!'

Margaret took a wad of banknotes from her purse. 'Here,' she said to Tamara as she handed over the money, 'a little money for you.'

All that could be heard was the rustle of banknotes and whisperings in Russian as Tanya and Tamara counted the money. Finally, Tamara spoke. 'You no' want show?'

'Give show to Tommy on the road,' Margaret said.

'*Da*, *da*, *da*,' the Russians said with one voice.

'Is good,' Tamara said. 'When we go?'

'Oh, Margaret!' Tommy said plaintively.

'Shut up!' Margaret said to Tommy. She turned to the girls. 'You go Friday night. Ferry sails from Lochboisdale at ten . . . at twenty-two hundred hours. You meet Tommy there at twenty-one hundred.'

'*Nyet*, *nyet*, *nyet*,' Tanya said. 'To-mee stay here. We entertain him.'

'Margaret, I'm begging you,' Tommy said, 'don't leave me with them.'

Margaret made a fist with her right hand and smacked it into the palm of her left. 'Tommy comes with me. You meet him Friday night at Lochboisdale.'

'Okay,' Tamara said seductively. 'To-mee, Friday night I let you feel my muscles, eh?'

'Let's go, Margaret,' Tommy said. 'Listen, give me a loan of your mobile, will you? I've got to phone somebody before I leave . . . that's if I have to leave.'

'Right,' Margaret said, handing over the phone. She turned towards the Russians. 'Tommy make call on telephone?'

Tommy had just got outside when he heard Tanya and Tamara chanting indoors. 'We . . . want . . . To-mee, we . . . want . . . To-mee.'

Tommy walked a short distance from the crofthouse and began to press buttons. Once through, he began to speak rapidly. 'No, I don't care to leave my name. Pick up a pen and stop faffing around.' There was a slight pause. 'George,' he said, 'good that I caught you in. What do you mean, who's this? This is Tommy. Remember you wanted a name? Well, this is it: Calum Macdonald from Garryhillie . . . Yeah, a Morris Minor, registration ST147X, eight Nine-Bars.' There was a delay of two seconds. 'I don't know who's goin' to be buying. You follow him, you'll find out, I suppose . . .' He listened for a while. 'You're welcome, George. It's a pleasure to do a favour for a friend with a good memory.'

The front door opened and Margaret emerged. She shouted over her shoulder, 'By-ee, by-ee.'

'By-ee, by-ee,' Tanya and Tamara called from inside.

When Margaret reached the spot where Tommy was standing she held out her hand to retrieve the mobile.

'There you go, Margaret,' Tommy said. 'Thank you. Guy wasn't in.'

'Everybody's so busy nowadays,' Margaret said. 'Aren't they, To-mee?'

14

He who is always jumping about will eventually fall over the cliff

Calum Macdonald shifted in the driver's seat of the Morris Minor, the little van rushing through the night, the hills and lochs appearing in the headlights far ahead and vanishing almost at once into the darkness. Suddenly, at Eochar road-end, just as he was approaching the south ford, he heard the wail of a police car behind him. He brought the van to a halt, pulled on the handbrake and shut off the engine.

The police car halted about a yard behind him and two men got out. One of the policemen rapped on the driver's window. The other stood at the rear of the van.

'Open your window,' the policeman said.

Calum rolled down the window. 'What's up?'

'Reckless driving, Calum,' said the policeman.

'Well,' said Calum, 'amn't I the stupid one? I thought you were in the wrong the way you were driving. Your car almost went up my arse back there.' He smiled scornfully. 'How'd you know my name?'

'We know a lot about you, Calum,' the policeman said. 'In my opinion, anybody who's driving on the main road in an old rust-bucket is nothing but an object of shame, an object of pity and a laughing-stock.'

'And where exactly,' Calum said, 'in your *How to Be a Policeman* manual is that written down?'

'Isn't written down anywhere,' the policeman said. 'I keep it in my head.'

'Is that right?' Calum said.

'Get out of the van,' the policeman said.

'Hey!' Calum said as he came out of the van, slamming the door behind him.

'Put your hands on the roof,' the policeman said, 'and shift your feet back a bit. Don't move.'

'What the fuck's happening here?' Calum said.

The policeman shouted to his colleague, 'Donald, open the rear door.'

'You guys got a warrant?' Calum said.

'No,' the policeman said, 'but Donald's got a big crowbar. Go for it, Donald.'

Calum heard the clash of metal on metal as Donald attacked first the door, then the locks on the cases. An angry frown appeared on his face. 'Hey,' he shouted, 'you can't do that!'

'We're doing it, boy,' the policeman said. He walked past Calum and made for the rear of the van. 'And what do we have here?' He spoke softly to Donald. 'How many packets, Donald?'

Donald poured out all the packets on to the floor of the van and spoke slowly. 'One . . . two . . . three . . . I think about . . . he's got nearly eighty ounces, George.'

'I'm placing you under arrest,' George said. 'Before

we ask you any questions, we want you to understand your rights.'

'I know my rights,' Calum said.

'Be quiet and listen to the man,' Donald said.

'You do not have to answer any questions,' George said. 'You have a right to remain silent. If you answer any questions, your answers may be used in evidence in court. Do you understand what I've just said to you?'

'Of course I understand,' Calum said. 'You think I'm a fuckin' idiot?'

'You took the very words out of my mouth,' Donald said.

'You have the right to the services of a lawyer,' George said. 'Do you have a lawyer?'

'Jesus, no,' Calum said. 'How would I have one of them? You just arrested me a minute ago.'

'If you want a solicitor,' George said, 'you need only say so, and we will give you time to engage a solicitor and to be advised by him. You are entitled to confer with your solicitor before you answer any questions. Do you understand what I've just said to you?'

'I understand,' Calum said.

'If you can't afford a solicitor,' George said, 'a solicitor will be appointed for you by the court. Do you understand that?'

'Yes,' Calum said.

'You may,' George said, 'if you wish, waive these rights and answer any questions we put to you. Will you answer questions?'

71

Calum said mockingly, 'You can show me your arse, and there's no way I'll answer.'

'Get in your vehicle,' George said. 'In the back seat. Donald, you get in with him. Keep a firm grip on him. If he moves, belt him one with your crowbar.'

George took out his phone and began to speak immediately. 'Iain? George here. Tell the sergeant we grabbed your man, that he had the stuff in the back of the van. We're coming in now.'

15

Lord! Things are going wrong!

'What a bampot he is!' Davy said to Duncan. They were seated at a table in the Borrodale Hotel at Daliburgh crossroads. A woman was singing a country & western song in the lounge, but with the uproar that surrounded them, from men chatting loudly and the constant rattling of glasses, they could not make out the melody or the words.

'You know who he phones from the police station?' Davy said. 'Me. Well, he called Alina, and he gets her and the kids up and she's pissed off and I had to give the police my name before they'd let him speak to me.'

'You told me he'd got better,' Duncan said.

'Better than who?' Davy said. 'Peter Manuel? Hannibal the Cannibal? He's goin' to be the death of me, that's what's goin' to happen.'

'Nice boy,' Duncan said.

'Ah,' Davy said, 'what he needs is a lawyer. I said to him, "Calum, I'll get you a lawyer. I can't do any more for you."'

'What good's a lawyer goin' to do him?' Duncan said.

'It'll do me some good,' Davy said. 'It'll get Calum off my back.'

'It'll be tough getting a good one who'll take Calum on,' Duncan said.

'In the name of God,' Davy said, 'I know I can't get a good one. Calum was alone when he got caught, and the stuff was in the back of the van. What's a lawyer goin' to do? Make the stuff disappear? The fellow Calum really needs is Paul Daniels.'

'You got the money to pay a lawyer?' Duncan said.

'No,' Davy said. 'I was just . . . how are you fixed yourself, Duncan?'

'Davy, I'm absolutely tapped out just now,' Duncan said. 'Do you know this? Something must have happened to the Russian girls, because I haven't received a brown penny from them since . . . I think it was, the last money I got was the day before yesterday . . . Monday . . . yeah.'

'It's the Elder that done it,' Davy said. 'That crazy bugger has been raping and pillaging in North Uist, and he's making his way south even as we blether here.'

'Those poor souls,' Duncan said.

'Well,' Davy said, 'I mean, we half expected something like this to happen.'

'We took our chances,' Duncan said.

'Right,' Davy said, 'and the Elder is now taking his time, like a thief in the night. Tell me what we should do, will you?'

'The Elder doesn't worry me,' Duncan said. 'Heard a

kind of mixed-up whisper about him today.' He sighed.
'Tell me, is he a kind of shy person?'

'Shy?' Davy said. 'He's about as shy as a streaker.
Why do you ask?'

'Seems like he doesn't like to be amongst people,'
Duncan said. 'Hasn't left his hotel room since he arrived
in Uist.'

'I'm not all that sure, Duncan,' Davy said. 'I'll send
Alina's wee girl to the door, I hear anyone knocking
during the night.' He shook his head. 'We goin' to carry
on with this other thing? "Conversation without
Bounds", remember?'

'As far as I can see it's looking good,' Duncan said.
'I've already written a couple of scripts. It won't be long
before you become really slick with them. But if you
don't want to do it, I'll get somebody else.'

'You'll have to excuse me, Duncan,' Davy said. 'I
don't much feel like doing anything just now. I'm
between a rock and a hard place. Like the old fellow
from Barra, I'm in a "quadrangle".'

16

The Elder's breakdown

The Elder stood in the middle of his hotel room in the
Dark Island Hotel in Benbecula, and from the red flush
on his face he was very angry indeed. Between hands as
big as shovels he shook the whisky bottle.

'This's empty,' he said. 'I've got another one somewhere.' He whipped a pillow off the bed and seized a full
bottle of Grouse. 'Here it is. Fancy a wee nip, Margaret?'
He gave no invitation to the ragged boy who stood in the
open doorway. He wrenched off the bottle top and filled
a half-pint tumbler with whisky.

'Too early for me,' Margaret said, seated on a padded
chair next to the television set.

'Too early?' the Elder said. 'It's nearly quarter to
ten.'

'Still too early,' Margaret said. 'You carry on if you
want a dram, though.'

'Excuse me, lady,' the young man said, 'you goin' to
pay me for . . . well . . . umh, the stuff?'

'No,' Margaret said.

The young man stared at her. 'You tinker!' he said.
'I thought you were kidding me on.'

'I never kid anybody on,' Margaret said. 'Ask the man from Lewis for the money.'

'That wee dwarf's looking for money, is he?' the Elder said. 'Bastard. If I give you the back of my hand, there'll be nothing left of you except your shoes.'

'Murdo,' Margaret said, 'whatever it was he sold you, you've got to pay him.' 'Half a quarter I gave you,' the lad said. 'Fifteen pounds, man.'

'Your gear's lousy, boy,' the Elder said. 'There'd be more kick in an Oxo cube. Come to think about it, maybe it was an Oxo cube.'

'No, no,' the lad said.

'Murdo,' Margaret said, 'pay him.'

'On the dressing table,' the Elder said, 'my wallet's on the dressing table.'

'Let him go,' Margaret said. 'I want to talk to you.'

'Hey, boy,' the Elder said, 'there's forty-three there. When I get up, I hope there's thirty-three there. Got that?'

The young man walked over to the dressing table, picked up the wallet and took out ten pounds. 'Okay,' he said, 'but amn't I getting a tip?'

'No,' the Elder said.

The young man twisted his head round and looked at the man from Lewis with mingled boredom and displeasure. 'That wasn't your tune at half past five this morning.'

'I'll give you a tip, then,' the Elder said. 'Get a proper job.'

'This is better than cutting peat,' the young man said.

'I wouldn't know anything about that,' the Elder said. 'It's oil-fired central heating we've got in Back.'

The young man walked towards the door. He halted. He turned to face the Elder. 'Well,' he said, 'it's not much better than cutting peat, sometimes. But it's, it's mostly better. The odd time, you know, you meet an old skinflint, and then it's mostly slower.' He turned.

'You know what, boy?' the Elder said. 'Some day an old skinflint's goin' to give you a punch that'll level you. How'd you like that?'

'You think it'd give me a bigger thrill than the Oxo cube?' the young man said.

'Fuck off, you prick,' the Elder said.

'Go to hell,' the young man said, and quickly departed, slamming the door behind him.

The Elder filled his glass again and drank a mouthful. He said to Margaret with sadness in his voice, 'Which is the very place I've been since I arrived on this island. I've been stuck in here since last Tuesday, and the only people I'm seeing are thieves. One worse than the other. And I've spent a fortune on . . . Oxo.'

'Are you goin' to be all right for Sunday?' Margaret said. 'Today's Thursday. You don't have much time.'

'I'm as fit as a fiddle, right now,' the Elder said. 'Christ's sake, leave me alone, will you?'

'I've changed my mind,' Margaret said. 'Don't go near the Russian girls. They're no longer involved in the business. What you'll do is, you'll go after this man, Tiny MacCormack, and when you're finished you'll put

78

the fear of death into Davy. Can you do that? I'm not goin' to cut your wages.'

'That's all right with me,' the Elder said.

'Look, Murdo,' Margaret said, 'this afternoon three guys are going to come up to your room here and they'll talk to you about what you've got to do. They'll take you on a trip.'

'Where the fuck are they?' the Elder said. 'Get them up here.'

'You,' Margaret said, 'I'll tell you what you're going to do, right? You're going to bed.'

'I'm not tired,' the Elder said.

'You look completely wiped out to me,' Margaret said. 'Go to bed, you clown. It's not even eleven o'clock yet. These people will come and visit you round about three and you better be up, because if you're not, I'm going to telephone Stornoway and the folk up there'll put your backside on a burner.'

'Okay,' the Elder said.

'No drink, no smoking, no nothing,' Margaret said. 'Get yourself a shower and get into bed. You understand?'

'I don't take orders from anyone,' the Elder said, 'never mind the likes of you, you bitch.'

17

When bad things happen, they happen with a vengeance

Margaret switched off the ignition of the Land-Rover and waited until MacAskill came out of the bank in Lochmaddy. As soon as he got in he started to speak right away. 'I'm not complaining, but do you know that you put over a hundred miles on the mileage when I lent you this vehicle the day before yesterday?'

'Get over it,' Margaret said. 'There'll be a lot more on the mileage before the weekend. I need it tomorrow as well.'

'What a time you're taking with this, girl!' MacAskill said. 'Okay, I'm here. What bad news do you have for me now?'

'Well,' Margaret said, 'it seems that we have . . . umh, we had a problem with the Lewisman.'

'We're not supposed to have *any* problems,' Mac-Askill said. 'What's up?'

'The Elder,' Margaret said. 'He's absolutely useless. I got rid of the Russians myself. Well, by tomorrow night they won't be around. I've an idea we won't be hearing from Mr Macdonald for a while . . .'

'What about Davy?' MacAskill said.

'Let me finish,' Margaret said. 'I'm pretty sure I can lay my hands on him whenever I want, but Tiny, I can't get near him just now.'

'But he's the main man,' MacAskill said. 'Won't the Elder do the business with him?'

'He can't,' Margaret said. 'If he was the Elder I knew a long time ago, he could do the business. But now, he's just a broken reed.'

'What's wrong with him?' MacAskill said.

'First thing,' Margaret said, 'he's drinking like a fish. Also he's become seriously fond of the ganja.'

'What did you say, girl?' MacAskill said.

'Ganja . . . gear . . . cannabis . . . marijuana, you know?' Margaret said.

'Oh, I get it,' MacAskill said.

'Anyway,' Margaret said, 'he's been in trouble with the law over some underage girl, he's not working, the wife's got a toy boy, and he's got hassle with his own kids. And he's no longer an elder.'

'That wouldn't prevent him doing the job for us here though, would it?' MacAskill said.

'It would,' Margaret said. 'He won't come out of his room.'

'Why?' MacAskill said.

'Paranoia,' Margaret said. 'When he landed in Benbecula he asked me to get him a lump of gear, and I thought, it's not my business. I spoke to a guy, the guy got him some stuff. What the Elder did then, he gets the guy to tell him what other people are in the same

81

business. Cannabis and whisky, that's what's kept him alive since he arrived.'

'The Elder has to leave Uist,' MacAskill said. 'It'd have been good if he'd left yesterday.'

'Three o'clock today, actually,' Margaret said.

'What?' MacAskill said.

'He was captured by three guys from the great Church of Back at three o'clock,' Margaret said.

'How?' MacAskill said.

'I phoned them,' Margaret said. 'Told them that he was demented and that he'd be better off amongst his own people on his death-bed.'

'And they took him away without any trouble?' MacAskill said.

'As soon as he clocked those crows, he left with them like a little lamb. I watched the four of them leaving. Know what the tall, skinny one said as they crammed him into the car? "Come along, Murdo," he said, "Christ's Gospel is a mystery to them here in Uist." '

'Maybe he wasn't far wrong,' MacAskill said. 'Okay, that leaves Tiny and the young fellow, Davy.'

'I came up with an idea just a minute ago,' Margaret said. 'I think I can get close to him.'

'I thought you couldn't,' MacAskill said. 'You didn't know where he'd be.'

'Davy,' Margaret said, 'I bet he knows where Tiny is going to be, tomorrow afternoon or tomorrow night.'

'Will he tell you?' MacAskill said.

'Yes,' Margaret said. 'I think I know a way of finding out where he'll be pretending to be Clint Eastwood, smoking his Hamlets and making his eyes all squinty.'

'There'll be no disturbance, though,' MacAskill said.

'Oh, it's hard to tell,' Margaret said.

'But this'll all be over soon, won't it?' MacAskill said.

'Mr MacAskill,' Margaret said, 'everything will be over tomorrow night at ten o'clock, promise. If it's not, tell you what I'll do, I'll let you take me out to dinner.' She smiled. 'In Maxim's in Paris.' She spoke softly in his ear. 'And I'll not say a word to Mary about it.' She took his face between her hands and gave him a kiss. 'Mmmmm.'

She shoved MacAskill out of the Land-Rover, started the engine and moved off.

MacAskill trotted after her. 'Stop, Margaret, stop,' he shouted.

Margaret stuck her head out the window and said sweetly, 'Come on, MacAskill, you need a little exercise. Don't want you having a heart attack.'

'I think I'm having a heart attack right now,' Mac-Askill said.

18

Women are often cunning

Davy sat on a bench-seat in reception in Creagorry Hotel, a pint of lager on the table in front of him. It was about five in the afternoon.

Margaret hung her coat on a hook beside the door and sat down beside him. She ordered a glass of white wine.

'You mind if I sit here?' Margaret said.

'No, indeed,' Davy said.

'Not many in at this time,' Margaret said.

'No,' Davy said, 'I prefer it like that. I come in here every day.'

'I know,' Margaret said.

'I've never seen you in here before,' Davy said. 'I don't know you.'

'Didn't say you did,' Margaret said. 'Not many know me here. I'm just a lawyer, that's all. I've never been in here before in my life.'

'What made you come in today?' Davy said.

'Looking for you,' Margaret said. 'I was looking for you and this guy told me you come in here a lot round about this time of day. So I came in. Simple, eh?'

'What guy's this?' Davy said.

'Friend of yours,' Margaret said. 'Well, he's the friend of somebody you know pretty well.'

'What's his name?' Davy said.

'Tommy,' Margaret said.

'Don't know anybody by that name,' Davy said. He gulped down about a quarter of his pint. 'I better be goin'.'

'Tommy'll be surprised at that . . . Calum too,' Margaret said.

'You know what happened to Calum?' Davy said.

'Yes,' Margaret said. 'Now, why don't you relax for a minute, Davy, okay? Have another pint. Oh, you've got a motor-bike, too, I understand.'

'Yeah,' Davy said.

'Suzuki Bandit 600,' Margaret said. 'Petrol tank painted orange?'

'Right,' Davy said.

'You smoke?' Margaret said.

'Just Marlboro,' Davy said.

'Well, that's good,' Margaret said. 'You want to be careful about that. The police are mustard on people who use the other stuff. As our Calum knows, eh? You've been out of the university, what, a year?'

'Eighteen months,' Davy said.

'Right,' Margaret said. 'Sociology, that right?'

'Yeah,' Davy said.

'Good for you,' Margaret said. 'It's good that you don't smoke these spliffs. You don't want the police after you, do you?'

'No,' Davy said, moving uncomfortably on the couch.

'And they're not going to come after you,' Margaret said, 'because you haven't done anything wrong, am I right?'

'Just having a pint in the pub,' Davy said.

'Certainly,' Margaret said, 'there's nothing wrong with that. You must have done some growing up, man.'

'Well,' Davy said, 'I finally got myself a girlfriend.'

'That's good,' Margaret said. 'How is she?'

'She's not all that good,' Davy said. 'Tell the truth, she's pretty rotten. She won't go to bed with me. But I'm goin' to keep at it, though, till I get someone who will. It seems that there are a lot of them about, it's just that I'm not meeting them.'

'That's the boy,' Margaret said. She made a tutting sound with her tongue and front teeth. 'God, that's a shame. If I'd have met you sooner, I know a girl who could've been a great help to you in that line of work. Unfortunately, she's leaving Uist tonight.'

'Yeah?' Davy said.

'Yeah,' Margaret said. 'That's really terrible. You maybe heard of her. Tamara MacIsaac. Beautiful girl. A beautiful, big girl, and she's off to Germany tonight. Her and her pal, Tanya.'

'Couldn't have got a husband in Uist,' Davy said.

'Maybe,' Margaret said, 'but I heard she actually had a husband in Uist.'

'You don't say,' Davy said.

'And that the other one, Tanya, was married to Calum Macdonald,' Margaret said.

'I think I'll have another pint,' Davy said.

'Well, now,' Margaret said, ignoring him, 'it seems they moved into this house in Strumore that belonged to an old woman but is now in the name of a man from South Uist. He's called Duncan MacCormack. Oh, boy, they used to have these wild parties every night of the week – booze, music and menfolk, you know? – and every morning one of them would come to South Uist with a parcel full of banknotes.'

'Wow!' Davy said.

Margaret lowered her voice. 'Where's he going to be tonight?'

'Who?' Davy said.

'Duncan MacCormack,' Margaret said. 'Tonight, where's he going to be?'

'I don't know,' Davy said.

'Davy, lad,' Margaret said, 'it's high time you started thinking about yourself. I'm quite willing to help you, but you've got to make an effort yourself.'

'This is the first time I've seen you,' Davy said.

'New friends are best,' Margaret said. 'That fellow, Tiny, you can't depend on him. Remember Tralee.'

'I don't know who the fuck you are,' Davy said.

'Not many people know me,' Margaret said. 'Oh, the Elder, and, oh yeah, George the policeman. George knows me. You want me to phone him, you can talk to him, find out some more about me?'

'No,' Davy said.

'Okay,' Margaret said, 'where's he going to be to-night?'

'I haven't got any idea,' Davy said. 'I've only seen

87

Duncan two or three times since I came back to Uist. I don't know what he does at night. He'll be at home, I suppose.'

'Okay,' Margaret said. She finished her wine. 'I'll be seeing you, Davy lad. I've got to speak to George.'

'Wait a minute,' Davy said.

'Why?' Margaret said. 'You tell me you don't know. Okay, I accept that.'

'Where Duncan's goin' to be tonight,' Davy said, 'is that what you want me to tell you?'

'Listen, sunshine,' Margaret said, 'Calum's in jail. There's two ways I can go with this. The hard way: the pair of you, you and Duncan, go to jail along with Calum. The other way: only one of you goes.'

Davy started to stutter. 'I'm . . . Jesus, I don't know.'

'Right,' Margaret said, 'make your choice, and make it right now.'

'Let me think . . .' Davy said.

'No,' Margaret said. 'Heads or tails, right now. I've got to go.'

'I don't know . . . I don't know if I can do this,' Davy said.

'Can you do the other thing?' Margaret said. 'The jail?'

Davy chewed his lips, all the time constantly rubbing his palms on his trousers. 'No.'

'Well,' Margaret said, 'looks like you've made your choice, then.'

'What've I got to do?' Davy said.

'Find out where he's going to be tonight,' Margaret said.

'I know that already,' Davy said. 'He's going for a swim in the pool at Liniclate School. Sometime between five and six. He's goin' to phone me or something. I told him I'd be in all night.'

'You're not going to be,' Margaret said.

'I'm not?' Davy said.

'No,' Margaret said.

'Where am I goin' to be?' Davy said.

'You're going to be with me,' Margaret said, 'and we're going to be where he's going to be – in the pool.'

'Holy Mother,' Davy said, 'I can't do that.'

'Okay,' Margaret said, 'you've made the other choice, then.'

'He'll see the two of us together and he'll know right away something's wrong,' Davy said.

'But we've got a chance to put things right,' Margaret said. 'Davy, you've got a chance to get on the right track after this.'

'What do you mean?' Davy said.

'You could go in for the law,' Margaret said. 'I've got my own practice in Edinburgh and we're always looking out for young people who'd make good trainees. Think about it. Now, we'd best make for Liniclate School.'

'Will I follow you on the motorbike?' Davy said.

'Leave it here,' Margaret said. 'Jump into the Land-Rover with me.'

'Okay,' Davy said.

Margaret snatched her coat and headed for the door, Davy hurrying behind.

19

'White they'll never be,' said the crow as she washed her feet

Margaret and Davy stood on the tiled flooring that surrounded the swimming pool in Liniclate School. The place was noisy with the constant lapping water and the shouts and squeals of children. Margaret observed Duncan closely as he swam closer and closer to the end of the pool where she and Davy were standing. Just as he touched the pool wall, she knelt down and seized his ear.

'Hi, Duncan,' Margaret said, 'what a good swimmer you are! Of course all sharks are good in the water.'

'Hi,' Duncan said breathlessly. He spat water. 'Who's this, Davy?'

Davy licked his lips before answering. 'This is . . . umh, I don't know what she's called . . . She's, this is my new boss, Duncan. You'd better listen to her.'

'Okay,' Duncan said, 'make it quick, girl. I don't have much time.'

'You don't have any time, Duncan,' Margaret said. 'The game's up.'

'What do you think you are – a referee?' Duncan said.

'You're not far wrong,' Margaret said. 'I'm a lawyer.'

'I absolutely detest lawyers,' Duncan said, 'and I don't think I like you either, sweetie.'

'What my friends think of me, that's what matters to me,' Margaret said. 'You don't like me, that's fine. I couldn't care less.'

'I can hardly wait to hear what you've got to say,' Duncan said.

Margaret pretended not to have heard him. 'I want everything to be fair and square on Lord Granville's estate in North Uist. They're not – far from it.'

'Oh, sorry to hear that,' Duncan said. 'It won't do to have one of old Liz's cousins all upset. What's your biggest problem?'

'You,' Margaret said.

'God,' Duncan said, 'I didn't even know that a lawyer would be acquainted with the likes of me.'

'But I am acquainted with you,' Margaret said, 'and unless you do as I say, a legal person who's far more important than me is going to get acquainted with you as well: the Sheriff.'

'She knows everything, Duncan,' Davy said.

'She knows nothing,' Duncan said. 'Maybe about you, but she can't harm me.'

'First of all,' Margaret said, 'I make reference to the croft in Strumore. The one that belonged to Kirsty. You made that poor old woman sign a document that transferred the place to you. "Extortion of Assignation of Tenancy", Duncan. Three years, at least. "Conspiracy to Circumvent Her Majesty's Immigration Laws",

91

Duncan. Another two years. "Living on Immoral Earnings", Duncan. They'll seize everything that belongs to you – houses, vehicles, every bank-book you ever possessed – then you'll get a massive fine and another stretch in prison.'

Duncan hauled himself out of the pool and stood facing the other two, his body dripping water and an expression of indignation on his face. 'Look, I'm sorry we had to meet like this.'

'You're nowhere near as sorry as I am,' Margaret said.

'Or as I am,' Davy said.

Duncan opened his mouth but no sound emerged for a full two seconds. 'But surely you could forget about this . . . umh, for a small, quick consideration of some kind?'

Margaret burst out laughing. 'Small? Quick? You're not underrating yourself, Duncan, are you?'

There followed an awkward pause. Finally, Duncan turned towards Davy.

'Davy, away and get me a towel.'

'I'm no longer with you, Duncan,' Davy said. 'I'm with her now.'

'I've told you what's going to happen,' Margaret said, 'and you don't like it. I'll tell you now what I can do for you. You can take it or leave it.'

'I'm almost on the point of desperation,' Duncan said through chattering teeth. 'I'll take anything.'

'Oh, I know that,' Margaret said, 'but there's a little more than taking something involved in this. This is a deal. You have to give something, right?'

'Right,' Duncan said in a feeble voice.

'I'll throw these complaints against you into the fire,' Margaret said, 'and I won't say a word to the police.'

'I'm not leaving Uist,' Duncan said.

'Duncan,' Margaret said, 'I'm not asking you to do anything.' She prodded his chest with her forefinger. 'I'm telling you.'

'But I've got to do something,' Duncan said.

'Correct,' Margaret said. 'Give me your solemn word: you'll not set foot on North Uist ever again. You can do all the depredation you like in South Uist but steer clear of North Uist.'

'Okay,' Duncan said with some reluctance.

'I'm not finished yet,' Margaret said. 'Sign this.' She took a bundle of papers from her bag along with a pen and watched Duncan as he scribbled. When he finished, she took the papers from him and put them back in her bag.

'What documents are these?' Davy said.

'They're to do with the house in Strumore,' Margaret said. 'I've got power of attorney over Kirsty's affairs now, and the croft's mine.' She inclined her head to Davy's ear and whispered, 'It'd make a terrific bachelor pad for some young guy – a kind of dacha in the country for him while he's working in the city, know what I mean?'

'Stop your blethering there,' Duncan said. 'I'm freezing over here.'

'You certainly are, boy,' Margaret grinned. 'I can see that. I thought I was going to talk to a man when I came

93

in here.' She stared pointedly at his crotch. 'The nuns in Daliburgh Hospital won't be able to help you. You'd be better off going to Yorkhill in Glasgow – to the Sick Children's Hospital.'

This brought a laugh from Davy. 'Isn't she funny, Duncan?' he said.

'Terribly amusing,' Duncan said dryly.

'Have we got an agreement?' Margaret said.

'Yeah,' Duncan said, his chin pressed down on his chest.

'There's a good lad,' Margaret said. 'Come here a minute till I give you a hug so that you can warm up a little.' She wrapped her arms around Duncan's body and began hugging him and patting him.

Duncan was obviously enjoying this. He panted and grunted.

Suddenly, Margaret forced him towards the edge of the pool. 'You'd better stay on this side of the ford from now on,' she said. 'I was really looking forward to turning you in.' Then she pushed him into the water.

Duncan tumbled backwards into the pool and made an enormous splash.

The children who had witnessed the struggle squealed with laughter.

in prison and if you want to train for a new profession in Edinburgh. You'll have those city girls pawing the ground for you. You'll have your Land-Rover. And because you're far too good-looking for a man, I'll have to fight them off to get into my own office in the morning.'

Davy fidgeted in the passenger seat. 'Of course, you're right. When I think about it, it's . . . well, it puts a different complexion on things.'

'That's good, Davy,' Margaret said. 'Now, I'll have to leave you, I've got a lot of phone calls to make tonight yet.' She got out of the Land-Rover, allowing Davy to slide across to the driver's seat. 'You know what you've got to do, now.'

'Yes,' Davy said brusquely. 'I make for Lochboisdale. To the pier. The others'll be waiting for me there. I don't stop at the hotel. You'll look after my motorbike for me till I come back.'

'I'll do that, my boy,' Margaret said. 'You're all right now, are you?'

'Yeah,' Davy said.

'Just making sure,' Margaret said. 'You couldn't drive properly back there.'

'I've got two hours to get up there,' Davy said. 'I'll take it easy.'

'You'll remember everything, won't you?' Margaret said.

'Yeah, yeah,' Davy said impatiently. 'Lochboisdale pier. I pick up Tommy and the hook – umh, the Russian lads and we're off to Germany.'

20

A dash down north

The Land-Rover leapt out of the parking space at Liniclate School, taking the bends on the road to North Uist at high speed with the tyres screaming. On the causeway between Benbecula and North Uist, Margaret said, 'You're going too fast, Davy.'

'Jesus,' Davy said, 'were you really going to tell on him . . . to the police, I mean?'

'Yes,' Margaret said. 'Of course I won't need to tell on you. One of them's going to catch us if you keep driving at this speed.'

'You live in Vallay, do you?' Davy said.

'Quite near,' Margaret said. 'Now, slow down.'

'I can't,' Davy said.

'Look, kid, slow down, you understand?' Margaret said.

'I can't,' Davy said. 'Honest to God, I can't.'

'We've got plenty time,' Margaret said.

'You want to drive?' Davy said.

'Yes,' Margaret said.

The Land-Rover came to an abrupt halt. Doors were opened, feet scurried around the car, and the doors were slammed shut. They took off, this time at a more leisurely pace.

'I hope,' Margaret said, 'you've calmed down by the time you've to take the Land-Rover back to South Uist.'

'Oh, have I got to take this back?' Davy said.

'Yeah,' Margaret said, 'you're going to Lochboisdale.'

'I am?' Davy said. 'What am I going to do about my motorbike?'

'Leave it where it is just now,' Margaret said.

'How do I get the Land-Rover back to you?' Davy said.

'I don't want it back,' Margaret said.

'What are you saying?' Davy said.

'It's a present I'm giving you, Davy,' Margaret said.

'For free?' Davy said.

'Put your hand in the glove compartment down there,' Margaret said. 'You'll find the documents – MOT, Certificate of Insurance, Registration Document and stuff like that. You can sell it when you've finished your business if you want.'

Davy opened the plastic folder and examined the contents. 'Oh, thanks a million. I'm really grateful to you . . . umh, what did you mean when you said "finished your business"? Is it when I reach Lochboisdale I'm clear?'

'Oh, no, Davy,' Margaret said, 'I'm afraid you've got to go a good bit further than Lochboisdale.'

'How far?' Davy said.

'To Hamburg,' Margaret said.

'I couldn't find my way to Castlebay never mind Hamburg,' Davy said.

'You'll be okay,' Margaret said. 'You've go guide.'

'Who?' Davy said.

'Tommy, my sister's boy,' Margaret said.

'But I don't know the man,' Davy said hard . . . umh, it won't be easy making co to a stranger on such a long journey. It's not hop between Uist and Germany, you know

'Oh, I know,' Margaret said, 'and so d Weren't he and Tommy over there a fortn

'I never heard anything about that at all.

'What a lawyer you're going to make, Da et said.

'How?' Davy said.

'You tell lies almost automatically,' M

'Well,' Davy said, 'I've got to say I'm going on a trip to Germany with a bugg guy I don't know.'

'It won't be just the pair of you,' 'There'll be folk you know very well tr

'What folk?' Davy said.

'Well,' Margaret said, 'your wife's g

'My . . . wife?' Davy said.

'Yeah, Tamara. She and her pal 7 both plenty of tender loving care Margaret stopped at her father's hous spoke for a good while.

Finally, Davy said resignedly, 'Do through with this?'

'Yes. That is if you don't want to

'Here,' Margaret said, handing him an envelope, 'take this.'

'What is it?' Davy said.

'A little money,' Margaret said. 'But the word people like us employ – lawyer-types, you know? – is "retainer".'

The Land-Rover door was closed with a bang. Davy moved off slowly, honking the horn enthusiastically.

21

Parting has to come

On Saturday morning, with an east wind rising, Margaret sat on a rock beside her father's gate and watched MacAskill as he approached, riding a bicycle.

When he got to where she was he spoke. 'Sorry I'm late.' He waved a hand towards the bicycle as an excuse. 'It's hard fighting against the wind.'

'Oh, aye,' Margaret said, 'as the old proverb says, "Come," said the King; "Stay, said the wind." '

'Don't I know it!' MacAskill said. 'My hands have gone numb coming here.'

'A good thing's well worth waiting for,' Margaret said.

'Everything's back to normal now, I take it,' MacAskill said. 'At long last.'

'Do you know this, MacAskill?' Margaret said. 'For a guy I'm trying to help, you're pretty grumpy. I could have had you come to Glasgow today to meet me. Have to go to Glasgow soon on business and I thought I'd go by plane today. I wouldn't have to come back until Monday. I'm trying to be nice to you.'

'What's wrong in Glasgow? War broken out between the Glaswegians and the Edinburgh folk?'

'It's a pretty straightforward thing,' Margaret said. 'This chap and his wife – they're singers, Eriskay Lilt they're called – they made a CD last year for a label in Glasgow and though they've sold almost fifteen hundred copies to date, they haven't received a brown penny up till now. I sent a long, brilliant letter to Glasgow saying I'll have their back teeth unless they send a cheque immediately. And if I take a trip down there, they'll regret it. I like to do a favour for folk now and again.'

'Do me a favour,' MacAskill said. 'As long as I live, don't do me a favour. I've seen how you work.'

'I'll tell you what to do,' Margaret said. 'Give me the money.'

MacAskill handed her a plump envelope and his eyes widened when she opened it and started to count the money. 'God,' he said, 'you're not going to do arithmetic out here?'

'Shut up,' Margaret said, mumbling as she continued to count.

'Happy?' MacAskill said.

'No,' Margaret said, 'there's only five thousand here.'

'Well,' MacAskill said, 'himself was saying, because you gave away the Land-Rover without permission . . . and because he didn't really have anything to do with the Elder . . . well, like, I thought it'd be appropriate to . . . hold on to three . . . until . . . well, umh, until I'd get a chance to speak to you.'

Margaret spoke harshly. 'Give me two thousand out of what you've got in the inside pocket of your jacket.'

'But, Margaret,' MacAskill said, 'that only leaves . . .'

'A thousand,' Margaret said. 'A grand because I didn't pay attention to business. It was me who hired the Elder and he was useless. That was my mistake. And I'm paying for it.'

'But the Land-Rover . . .?' MacAskill said in a pathetic voice.

'Tommy asked somebody at MacLennan's down at Balivanich what it was worth,' Margaret said, 'and the guy said he wouldn't give a cassette of Iain MacKay for it. Give me the two thousand.'

Without the slightest degree of pity in her eyes Margaret stared at MacAskill.

Eventually, he handed over a wad of notes. 'You're difficult to satisfy, woman.'

'Get out of my sight, you tightwad,' Margaret said, 'and I'll be satisfied then.'

'Margaret,' MacAskill said plaintively, 'I thought we were quite close. I imagined that we had something together.'

'Perhaps we had,' Margaret said, 'for a while.' She smiled. 'We really can't complain. That's life, Mister MacAskill. We possess something. But only for a brief time.'

MacAskill mounted his bicycle and got ready to ride away. 'Can I give you a lift anywhere?' he said.

Margaret had a broad smile on her face as she waved her hand in dismissal. 'If I want a lift, I'll phone for a taxi. Beat it, and pray to God I don't phone Mary.'